The Infinite Questions of Dottie Bing

DIAL BOOKS FOR YOUNG READERS
An imprint of Penguin Random House LLC, New York

First published in the United States of America by Dial Books for Young Readers, an imprint of
Penguin Random House LLC, 2023
Text copyright © 2023 by Molly B. Burnham
Illustrations copyright © 2023 by Fanny Liem

Visit us online at penguinrandomhouse.com.

Library of Congress Cataloging-in-Publication Data is available.

Printed in the United States of America

ISBN 9780593406663

1st Printing

LSCH

Design by Sylvia Bi and Jessica Jenkins
Text set in Janson Text LT Pro

To the amazing grandparents and to folks who act like grandparents; to Aunt Joannie, who loved Chock full o'Nuts; and most of all to Tom Greene, who could do many things, including but not limited to, taking his fake teeth out.

The Infinite Questions of Dottie Bing

by MOLLY B. BURNHAM
with illustrations by FANNY LIEM

Dial Books for Young Readers

1. Grandpa Walter?

The first thing Dottie saw when she opened the door was Grandpa Walter and the Chock full o'Nuts can.

Dottie was not expecting to see Grandpa Walter, much less the Chock full o'Nuts can.

It had been two months since she had seen either of them, and remembering that day always made her feel like she had swallowed an alligator.

(Nothing against alligators, but swallowing one did not feel good.)

"Mom!" Dottie shouted. "Grandpa Walter's here."

"Walter? Your grandfather?" Dottie's mom shouted back.

"What other Walter do you know?" Grandpa Walter hollered from the doorway. He had to lean around Dottie because she hadn't budged. It wasn't that she wanted to block him from coming inside. It was shock that made her body stop working.

The shock was from the disbelief that of all the days Grandpa

Walter might appear, he chose *today*. Most Thursday afternoons were not exciting. Most Thursday afternoons were simply the day after Wednesday and the day before Friday. But this one was different. This one had a plan. An *important* plan. In fact, the plan was so important that Dottie could call it a *mission*.

"Mission," Dottie whispered to herself. Why hadn't she thought of calling it a mission sooner? Sam would like that word. Now that Dottie thought about it, Ima would like that word too. And considering how important Ima was to the plan—*mission*— it was nice to think that she was happy.

Dottie's mom rushed over, slipped past Dottie, and swept Grandpa Walter into a hug. "Walter, you should have told us you were coming."

"I wanted to surprise you," Grandpa Walter said.

"Well, you did," Dottie's mom replied, laughing.

This was Grandpa Walter's first visit without Ima. Of course, in a way Ima was with him. Just in a really different way.

Dottie eyed the Chock full o'Nuts can and tried to swallow the alligator down.

Dottie's mom asked, "Does Frank know you're here?" Frank was Dottie's dad and Grandpa Walter's son.

"I wanted to surprise him too," Grandpa Walter said.

"He will be surprised." Dottie's mom smiled and nodded.

Dottie didn't mind who Grandpa Walter surprised as long as he didn't interfere with her plan. "I mean mission," Dottie said under her breath as Grandpa Walter walked into the house, bringing the Chock full o'Nuts can with him.

2. Who Is He Talking To?

Dottie," her mom said. "Bring Grandpa Walter's suitcase upstairs, will you? I'm going to call your dad." Dottie's dad was at the bakery where he worked.

The alligator was still squirming around in Dottie's neck, so she only managed to squeak and nod, which was good enough for Dottie's mom. Before picking up the suitcase, Dottie stuck her head outside. No sign of Sam Batty. That was a relief. Dottie didn't want to be late for the first day of her mission.

By the time Dottie reached the stairs, Grandpa Walter was already halfway up them—a second later, though, he stumbled and tripped.

This was not unusual for Grandpa Walter. He was a born klutz. He said so himself. He spilled food, broke glasses, fell off chairs, dropped plates, and he couldn't catch a ball to save his life. Ima found it charming. That's what she said every time. "Walter, you are charming."

And Grandpa Walter would smile a tiny, crooked smile that showed how much he loved being charming to Ima. And then he would say, "If I wasn't a klutz, we never would have met."

This was true. Dottie knew the story by heart because Ima loved telling it. And every time Ima got to the part where Grandpa Walter dumped spaghetti Bolognese all over her, she would laugh so hard, she would snort. Ima loved to laugh.

Ima always ended the story by saying, "Worst waiter, best husband."

Back on the stairs, Grandpa Walter let out a "Whoa!" as he grabbed the banister and then an "Uh-oh!" as the Chock full o'Nuts can flew out of his hands, and then an "Oh no!" as the can flipped through the air and landed right at Dottie's feet.

The last time she had seen the Chock full o'Nuts can was two months ago at Ima's memorial. This was the same day Dottie's alligator appeared and the day Dottie decided she never wanted to see the Chock full o'Nuts can again. Not because the can was creepy. (Dottie liked creepy stuff.) She never wanted to see the can again because it hurt too much.

And now, here it was, gently rocking side to side until finally coming to a complete stop. Dottie couldn't take her eyes off it.

Grandpa Walter trotted down. "Sorry about that," he said, scooping up the Chock full o'Nuts can.

With the can gone, Dottie swallowed the alligator down and said, "No need to be sorry, Grandpa Walter. It was just an accident."

Grandpa Walter looked confused and then said, "Oh, I wasn't talking to you, Dottie."

Dottie looked around for someone else he could be speaking to. There wasn't anyone here unless you counted the Chock full o'Nuts can, and who would count a can?

It was true that Dottie was only ten and didn't understand a lot of things. It was also true that she did not understand Grandpa Walter. *Not at all*. He was quiet and kept to himself. He didn't tell stories or play games with Dottie or ask her any interesting questions. He didn't watch TV with her or go see movies or read books to her. (In other words, he was nothing like Ima.)

He wasn't mean. He was just who he was: Grandpa Walter. And to Dottie, Grandpa Walter was a mystery.

But as mysterious as he was, Dottie was pretty sure not even *he* would talk to the Chock full o'Nuts can.

3. What's in the Can?

Dottie followed Grandpa Walter and the Chock full o'Nuts can up the stairs and down the hall to her room. Was the Chock full o'Nuts can going to stay in her room? She hadn't considered that until now. If it were a regular old can, she wouldn't have minded. Ima and Grandpa Walter's house was full of Chock full o'Nuts cans.

The cans held marbles, pennies, and plants. One sat next to the stove for fat drippings. Kitchen utensils filled another, while others held pens and pencils, rubber bands, and even decks of cards. It was Ima who had read the words to Dottie when she was too little. "*Chock full o'Nuts.*" Dottie figured if a can said *nuts* right in the name that there would be nuts inside.

She was wrong.

It turned out that those brightly colored yellow cans with the cheerful black and green lettering were filled with something else. Something horrible. Something that tasted like mud.

"It's not nuts," Ima had told her, and pointed to all the words on the can, including the small ones. "*Chock full o'Nuts*," Ima read. "*The Heavenly Coffee.*"

"Coffee?" Dottie gagged. "Yuck." Coffee would never be heavenly to Dottie, but Ima and Grandpa Walter drank it by the gallon.

But now there was a new can in town.

This can appeared at the celebration for Ima's life.

This can was filled with something that wasn't coffee.

This can was filled with Ima.

To be precise, this can was filled with Ima's ashes.

4. What's So Funny?

Dottie's room was the smallest in the house. There was just enough space for a tiny desk, a bureau, and a bed. The bed was small, but Ima and Grandpa Walter always slept there when they visited. Ima liked snuggling and cuddling and smooshing close together. "Dottie," she'd say. "Life is too short to waste being far away from people." And then, she'd squeeze right next to wherever Dottie was sitting. Even if it was on her lap!

On these visits, Dottie moved into her sister's room, which was larger than Dottie's. Jazzy was four and had the kind of personality that needed a lot of space. Dottie never loved moving out of her room, but she loved Ima so much that she almost didn't mind.

"Dottie," her mom said, poking her head in the door, the phone pressed to her ear. "I'm still trying to reach your dad. Could you clear out a few drawers so Grandpa Walter can put his clothes away?"

"Sam and I have a—" Dottie started to say, before her mom interrupted.

"Sam can wait."

Dottie disagreed, but the look on her mom's face told her not to say so.

Her mom disappeared down the hall and Dottie gathered up clothes out of her bureau, ran into Jazzy's room, dumped them on the floor, and then ran back. "There you go," she said.

Grandpa Walter nodded.

Dottie waited for Grandpa Walter to say something more, but he didn't. If Ima were here, she would have said something. Maybe even told a funny story about losing her suitcase, or else she would have given her a hug and said thanks. Grandpa Walter, though, was not a talker or a hugger.

"Well," Dottie said. "If you don't need anything else, I'll be—"

"Dottie." Her mom's head popped into the room again, the phone still in her hand. "Could you unpack Grandpa Walter's suitcase for him?" And she quickly walked away whispering into the phone before waiting for Dottie's answer.

Grandpa Walter sat on the edge of Dottie's bed with the Chock full o'Nuts can in his hands.

Again, Dottie wondered why he had brought the can. Why didn't he leave it at home? On a shelf. Where it should be.

Dottie frowned at Grandpa Walter's suitcase. She wished it were Ima's. She loved putting away Ima's things. Dottie and Ima turned it into a game. Ima gave clues and Dottie had to decide which clothes they were. Like, *I'm always with another.* (Socks.) Or, *I'm a house with four open windows.* (A sweater.)

The alligator stretched out in her throat. Dottie swallowed hard, trying to get it to move along. It didn't listen, which annoyed her and explained the ferocity with which she unpacked Grandpa Walter's clothes. (*Ferocity* was Sam's word.) Dottie couldn't recall what it meant but it sounded exactly how she felt. She pulled out five shirts, three pairs of slacks, three sweaters, seven pairs of socks, and one pair of sneakers.

All the normal stuff.

Then she got to his underwear.

Underwear is always funny. But Grandpa Walter's was *hilarious.*

It had puppy dogs on it and bow ties, coffee mugs and teapots. One pair had chili peppers and one was covered with hearts. Dottie knew about this underwear because Ima had given them to Grandpa Walter on his last birthday.

Everyone had laughed when he opened it—even Grandpa Walter—and then he produced a box for Ima. (Grandpa Walter always gave Ima a present on his birthday.) Ima opened it and pulled out underwear. Underwear with puppy dogs, bow ties, coffee mugs and teapots, chili peppers, and hearts. They had given each other the exact same present!

Ima had laughed so hard that she peed her pants, which made her laugh even more. Even now, just thinking about it made Dottie laugh.

Grandpa Walter looked over. "What's so funny?" he asked.

Dottie held up the underwear with hearts.

He nodded. "It's all I've got." The way he said this made it feel like he wasn't just talking about the underwear, but Dottie couldn't figure out what else he could mean.

When Dottie was finished putting away his things, Grandpa Walter stretched out on the bed and said, "Now we need a nap."

Dottie wasn't quite sure who else needed a nap except Grandpa Walter until he rested the Chock full o'Nuts can beside him.

Oh. Dottie didn't think a can needed a nap, but she wasn't about to ask. There was a mission to start.

5. Are You Kidding?

Sam Batty was waiting on Dottie's front yard when she finally ran outside. "I'm so sorry," she said, and then explained about Grandpa Walter's surprise visit.

"Is he okay?" Sam asked.

"He seems okay. Why wouldn't he be okay?"

Sam shrugged. "I don't know. It's just Grandpa Walter isn't the kind of grandpa that does surprises."

He had a point, but Dottie didn't want to discuss Grandpa Walter.

"Sam," she said seriously. "I have asked you here today because I have a plan—I mean mission."

"A mission," Sam said. "I like that word."

"I knew you would!" Dottie knew everything about Sam and Sam knew everything about Dottie.

Dottie knew Sam hated pickles. And Sam knew Dottie slept in socks.

Dottie knew that Sam hated sleepovers and Sam knew about the funny underwear.

Dottie knew that Sam was nervous about his mom having a new baby and what life would be like as a no-longer-only child.

And Sam knew that Ima was in the Chock full o'Nuts can.

Sam also knew how sad Dottie felt and how much she wanted it to stop.

Dottie shook these thoughts out of her head. There was a mission to focus on. Dottie took a deep breath and started telling Sam her idea.

"Before Ima got sick, she told me she always wanted a tree house but because she grew up in a city, she never had one."

Sam's eyes lit up. "She wanted a tree house? She was the best." Sam always loved visiting with Ima, and Ima loved visiting with Sam. Whenever she came to stay, she insisted on playing cards, just the three of them. (Ima loved playing cards.)

Dottie continued, even though the alligator was squeezing into her throat, making it hard to talk.

"She told me how she was sure that if there was a tree house to play in, she would have been the happiest kid in the world."

Sam nodded. "Ima was the smartest person I ever knew, so she's got to be right."

"And since I want to be happy," Dottie concluded, "I've decided we need to build a tree house."

Sam's eyes got big. "You want us to build a tree house?"

"Yeah."

"That's the mission?"

"Yeah."

"Just you and me?" Sam sked.

"Yeah."

"Without any grown-ups?"

Dottie hadn't actually thought about that part. "Is that a problem?" she asked. That's what Ima used to say to anyone who questioned her. Like asking for extra whipped cream on her ice cream or telling cashiers that she brought her own bag because she didn't want a plastic one.

"Is that a problem?" Sam repeated, a smile spreading across his face. "Are you kidding? That is definitely not a problem."

Sam's enthusiasm was one of the many reasons why he was Dottie's best friend. That, and how he didn't need help from grown-ups.

6. What's the Question?

So," Sam said. "What do we do first?"

"We start with choosing a tree."

"Well, that'll be easy," Sam said. "There's only one to choose."

Dottie's face lit up. "That's what I think too!" Dottie already felt happier. "There's only one tree that will work and it's that one." Dottie pointed.

"*That* one?" Sam asked. He didn't sound convinced.

The tree Dottie picked was the oldest tree in the neighborhood and grew in front of the oldest house in the neighborhood. It was huge with limbs that stretched out wide and could probably hold five tree houses.

"It's perfect." Dottie beamed.

"Is it?" Sam asked.

"It's the biggest," Dottie insisted.

"I don't think that matters," Sam said.

"It's got the largest branches."

"I don't think that matters either."

"It's been waiting for us all our lives."

"Hmmm, I'm not sure about that."

Dottie was getting annoyed. "Give me one reason why we can't build the tree house in it."

"Because it doesn't belong to us."

Dottie sighed. Sometimes Sam was so sensible. "But Sam, who would notice if we built a tree house in it?"

"Who would notice?" He waved his arms in every direction. "Dottie, look around. A better question is: Who wouldn't notice?" Sam had a point. The block they lived on was jam-packed with houses that were all the same size and shape.

The only house that was different was the one with the tree. It was brick, had two chimneys, and ivy creeped all over it—even over the windows. The front door sat smack in the middle of the house and windows were evenly placed on either side and above. It was said to be empty, but Dottie and Sam knew the truth. There was something inside that house. Maybe zombies. Probably zombies. Okay, *definitely* zombies. This was why Dottie and Sam called it Zombie House.

Dottie crossed her arms. "Are you worried about the zombies?"

"No, I'm not worried about the zombies," Sam said. "The problem with the tree is that it belongs to the house, and we do not own the house, *and* the house is across the street."

Dottie frowned. She hated it when Sam was right.

"There's only one tree we can use," Sam said, and dragged Dottie around the side of her own house. He pointed to the tree next to her bedroom window.

Dottie shook her head. "It's not big enough."

"It is," Sam Batty said.

"The branches are puny," Dottie said.

"It'll be great."

"It isn't even tall."

"It goes all the way up to your window," Sam Batty said.

"My window isn't very high."

Sam put his head into his hands. "I abdicate." Sam had just turned eleven but had the vocabulary of a ninety-seven-year-old.

"Abdinate?" Dottie asked. "What does that mean?"

"Ab-di-*cate*," Sam repeated. "It means I give up!"

"You can't give up!" Dottie exclaimed. "We haven't even started."

"And we never will if we don't have a tree."

Sam was right. But Dottie didn't want to build a tree house in just any old tree. This tree house was special. It deserved the very best tree.

"Look," Sam said. "I know this is important to you."

Dottie nodded. It was.

"But I have to ask: What would Ima say if she were here?"

This was not as unusual a question as it sounded. Dottie and Sam regularly asked each other this question. Ima was the smartest grown-up either one of them knew. Whenever there was a problem, Ima always said the same thing. "Remember every solution starts with a question." She would pause and then add, "The hard part is finding the right one."

So, what was the right question? Dottie thought it was: Which tree is best for a tree house? Obviously, that was Zombie Tree. But now she wondered if maybe that was the wrong question and the right question was: Which tree could they build a tree house in? If building the tree house was what mattered, then Dottie knew the answer. She took one last look at Zombie Tree. "We'll go with your tree," she said.

"Yes!" Sam said, leaping up. "This is going to be great, Dottie. Really great."

Dottie hoped so. She was on a mission and failure was not an option.

7. What Means "Better than Good"?

It was Sam's smart idea to draw what they wanted the tree house to look like before they built it. He said that's what architects did. (Sam wanted to be an architect when he grew up. Dottie was still deciding.) Sam and Dottie ran to his house and then returned to the tree with a bin full of markers, paper, scissors, glitter, and various other art supplies like tape and glue. Sam's mom was very organized. She had bins for everything.

"You draw the tree," Sam said.

It was hard to draw on the bumpy grass. Dottie wished she were in her room instead of down on the ground. It would have been easier, not only because of her desk, but also because she would have had a better view. There wasn't anything to do about that, so she tried her best.

After Dottie drew the tree, Sam drew a platform between the branches. Then together they added walls and a roof.

When this was done, they studied the drawing.

"In my head it looked a lot better," Dottie said.

"Mine too," Sam agreed.

They looked at the tree and then back at their drawing.

"What if we add a second floor?" suggested Sam.

"Yes!" Dottie said. "Two floors."

They taped another piece of paper to the top of their first one and continued to draw. It still wasn't right.

"How about a tower?" Dottie asked.

"I love towers," Sam said. They drew a tower, then stopped, scrutinizing it again.

"We can't get in without a door!" Sam pointed out. They both laughed. How could they have forgotten a door?

"How about a secret door?" Dottie suggested.

"What's a secret door?"

"I don't know, but I want one."

"Windows?" Sam wondered. They drew windows. "Could we also have a secret window?" he asked.

"Why not?" Dottie said. And they drew a couple of secret windows.

Sam grabbed a new piece of paper so they could draw the inside of the tree house. "We need a shelf." He drew the shelf.

"And a secret shelf to hide stuff!" Dottie drew that.

"And a bench to sit on," Sam said.

Something was still missing. What was it?

"A bubble machine?" Dottie proposed.

"A bubble machine is good, but I don't think that's the problem."

They stared hard at the drawing.

"Oh!" Dottie rolled her eyes. "We need a ladder." How could they get up and down without a ladder?

And all of a sudden, they were on a roll.

"We need a slide," Sam said.

"And a trapdoor," Dottie added.

"And a rope pulley."

"And don't forget a hammock!"

They colored the drawing until it was completely done, then took a step back.

"This is good," Dottie said.

"This is better than good," Sam said.

"What's a word that means 'better than good'?" Dottie asked. Sam loved words and Dottie loved using them.

Sam thought for a second and then said, "Majestic."

Dottie knew the word *majesty* because it was used to talk about kings and queens, but she didn't know *majestic*.

"*Majestic* means 'awe-inspiring,'" Sam explained.

"Majestic," Dottie repeated. She liked that word and knew that Ima would have liked it too.

8. Why Not?

When Dottie and Sam left each other, both their spirits were high. They had a mission, but even better, Dottie's alligator had vanished. She walked into the kitchen, expecting to see her dad cooking dinner, like always. Instead of her dad, though, she found Grandpa Walter chopping vegetables. The Chock full o'Nuts can was sitting on the counter next to him. Dottie's belly churned. Was that the alligator? It couldn't be.

"Let me make dinner." Dottie's dad stood next to Grandpa Walter looking helpless. "You've just arrived," he pleaded to his own dad.

"Absolutely not," Grandpa Walter said. "I surprised you and I will cook for you just like your mother would have done."

Dottie's dad drummed his fingers on the table. There wasn't much to do. It was true about how Ima cooked when she and Grandpa Walter visited.

"What are we having?" Dottie asked, changing the subject.

"Soup," Grandpa Walter said.

"Did someone say soup?" Jazzy asked as she cartwheeled into the kitchen. Since Jazzy had learned how to cartwheel it was her favorite way to get around. Except on the stairs because that was too dangerous.

"I love soup!"

"I love soup too," Grandpa Walter said.

Dottie did not love soup. It was too soupy. Ima never would have made soup. (She knew Dottie hated it.) Ima would have asked Dottie what *she* wanted and then would have made that.

"Dottie," Grandpa Walter said. "Why don't you and Jazzy set the table for dinner."

"Now?" Dottie asked. She had wanted to think about the tree house some more.

"No time like the present," Grandpa Walter said. This was something Ima used to say. Of course, when Ima said it, there were puddles to splash in, or flowers to smell, or a cake to bake. She never would say it for something as boring as setting the table. But Dottie and Jazzy did what he asked (although Jazzy did more cartwheeling than anything else).

When they were done, Grandpa Walter said, "Dinner is served." And everyone sat down. Everyone except Grandpa Walter, who hustled back into the kitchen and returned with the Chock full o'Nuts can, placing it beside him. "Well," he said, picking up his spoon. "Eat up. You don't want the soup to get cold."

Dottie felt the alligator wiggle in her belly. She did not like the can at the table. She did not *want* the can at the table.

Her parents clearly didn't want the can at the table either. She waited for them to say something, but they didn't.

"Oops," Grandpa Walter said, "I forgot the salt." He went back into the kitchen.

Jazzy took a big slurp of soup and then asked, "Why does Ima live in a can now?"

"Jazzy," Dottie's dad said. "We don't ask questions like that."

"Why not?" Jazzy asked.

Her dad sputtered trying to find an answer. "It's not polite," he said.

Dottie frowned. When Ima was still alive, she was constantly asking questions: Why does toast smell so good? How was butter invented? Who could make the tallest cookie tower? And, Dottie's all-time favorite, how many oranges could Ima juggle? (The answer was none, but she always tried.)

"Frank," Dottie's mom said. "She's four. Four-year-olds like to ask questions."

Dottie thought about this. "I'm ten," she said. "And I like to ask questions." It was one of the ways she and Ima were alike. Ima always said so.

"Sure you do," her dad said. "Mom isn't saying you don't."

"But," Dottie went on, "she said four-year-olds like to ask questions."

Jazzy said, "I just want to know why Ima lives in a can."

Dottie's mom leaned over. "Let's talk about it later."

Dottie closed her eyes. She didn't want to think about Ima in the can, or the alligator crawling up her neck, so instead she would think about questions. Questions. Questions. "What happens when Jazzy turns five?" Dottie blurted out. "Does she stop asking questions?"

Jazzy's eyes got big and she started to cry. "I don't want to turn five! I hate five. Five looks mad."

"How can a number look mad?" Grandpa Walter asked as he returned to the table with the salt.

"It's mad and angry and I don't want to turn five!" Jazzy wailed.

Grandpa Walter pulled out a pencil and a scrap of paper from his pocket and began scribbling.

"I AM NEVER TURNING FIVE!" Jazzy hollered, and leaped up from the table.

Dottie's mom followed, trying to calm Jazzy down and Dottie's dad trailed after to see if he could help.

This left Dottie, Grandpa Walter, and the Chock full o'Nuts can.

"I still don't understand how five is mad," Grandpa Walter said. "Oh, wait. Now I see it. A five does look mad. Do you see how a five looks mad?"

Dottie looked up, but Grandpa Walter wasn't talking to her. He was showing the paper to the Chock full o'Nuts can. (THE CHOCK FULL O'NUTS CAN!) Why was he showing anything to the can? It was a can. A can of ashes. Nothing else.

Her throat tightened as the alligator settled in like it was sinking into mud and planned to stay awhile.

Grandpa Walter returned to his dinner. "Eat up, Dottie, or your soup will get cold."

Even if she liked soup, she couldn't eat it. Swallowing was not an option until the alligator decided to move along. (And by the feeling in Dottie's neck, she didn't expect that to happen anytime soon.)

9. How Long Is Not Long?

After dinner, Grandpa Walter and the can headed upstairs to get ready for bed. Dottie's dad appeared a few minutes later and Dottie helped clear the table. They were almost done when Jazzy ran into the room. By the smile on her face, it was obvious she wasn't mad at the number five anymore.

"Top or bottom?" asked Jazzy.

Dottie put down the plate she was carrying. For Dottie, this was the worst question in the world. "Both bunks stink," Dottie said.

Jazzy shrugged. "Mom said you get to choose."

Dottie shook her head. A choice, she thought, should be good or bad. This one was just bad or bad. If she picked the bottom and Jazzy slept on top, she would never sleep. Jazzy tossed and turned, and the bed shook and creaked and then Jazzy's blankets always fell over the edge, tickling Dottie's face.

But if Dottie slept on the top and Jazzy slept on the bottom, then Jazzy bounced and tossed and turned so much that it felt like the bed was about to topple over and Dottie couldn't sleep.

How could one question be so impossible to answer? It was like trying to decide if you wanted to be chased by zombies or thrown into a pit of poisonous snakes. Either way, it was bad news.

In the end, Dottie chose the top bunk. She hated blankets tickling her face more than fearing for her life.

Dottie slept deeply until the middle of the night when she woke to find Jazzy spread out across her like a starfish. Dottie thought she knew everything about sleeping with Jazzy, but this was a first. Dottie climbed out of the bed, to finish the night in the bottom bunk.

The next time she woke, it was morning, and MacFurry was attacking her feet.

MacFurry was a pillow-sized fur-ball of a cat, whose sweet look hid the heart of a warrior cat.

Pugnacious. That was Sam's word. It was fun to say, but it meant he liked to fight. He had been that way as long as Dottie had known him, which was all her life. She worried that she was too late to save MacFurry from a life of pugnaciousness. Thankfully, Ima had told her that there was no such thing as too late. Not for a thank-you note. Not for a hug. Not even for un-pugnaciousing a cat. It only took patience and attention. And protection. (This explained why Dottie wore socks to bed every night and would always wear them—at least until the day MacFurry calmed down.)

It was Ima who suggested Dottie wear socks to bed. (Ima always had solutions to every problem.)

"Dottie!" her mom called from downstairs. "Time to get moving, or you'll be late!"

"Oops!" Dottie leaped out of bed and ran to the bathroom, colliding with Grandpa Walter.

"Won't be long, Dottie," he said, and slipped into the bathroom with the Chock full o'Nuts can tucked under his arm.

Dottie stood there as the door closed in her face. She didn't mind that Grandpa Walter was in the bathroom, but did he need to bring the Chock full o'Nuts can with him? Sure, he and Ima brushed and flossed their teeth together and they were often heard singing sea shanties in the bathtub, but taking the Chock full o'Nuts can in with him? That was surprising. Or as Sam would say, flabbergasting. That was a fun word.

To make the time go by faster while waiting for the bathroom, Dottie hopped from foot to foot, repeating the word *flabbergasting*. After she said "flabbergasting" twenty times in a row, the word sounded more like "glabberflaster," which was funny but didn't help Dottie, who now needed the bathroom so much that she had to stop hopping.

It seemed to Dottie that Grandpa Walter had been in there for a long time, which made her wonder whether her idea of not long was shorter than his. Or whether his idea of not long was longer than hers. It was so confusing how differently people saw the same thing.

Ima used to say, "You never know a person until you walk

in their shoes." Dottie was sure that even if she walked in Grandpa Walter's shoes, she would never know him.

Luckily, before she had to think much more about the bathroom or shoes or how much she needed to use the bathroom, the door opened, and Grandpa Walter walked out.

Dottie dashed in, making it to the toilet just in time.

10. Truth or Fake?

The first thing Dottie did when she arrived downstairs was check the clock. She and Sam walked to school together every day and he would be here any second.

"Meow," Jazzy said, and then explained to Dottie (who hadn't asked) why she was wearing cat ears. "It's dress like your favorite animal day. I'm MacFurry. Except, a nice MacFurry." She turned to her cereal bowl and lapped the milk up with her tongue.

Dottie meowed back, and rubbed the top of Jazzy's head. Just then, the doorbell rang. Sam! Dottie grabbed her lunch and hugged her mom goodbye.

"Meow!" Jazzy shouted at her.

"Meow," Dottie shouted back as she sprinted to the door, flinging it open to find Sam on the other side.

Sam had moved in next door five years earlier—the day before the first day of kindergarten. Dottie was not excited about kindergarten and the next morning she refused to get dressed. She refused to put on her shoes. She refused to eat breakfast. And she refused to answer the door when the bell rang. There was no way she was going to kindergarten, and no one was going to make her. But then the doorbell rang again, and when her mom opened it, Sam was there, asking to walk to school with Dottie. And suddenly Dottie had a friend and kindergarten didn't sound so bad.

That's how they became best friends. That was the same day Sam told the class that he was he and to stop calling him she. That was also the day Dottie wore pajamas to school because she hadn't had time to change. It was a surprisingly great first day of kindergarten.

Kindergarten was also when Dottie and Sam made up their game Truth or Fake. It was such a good game that five years later they still played it.

"Truth or fake?" Dottie asked as they walked along. "If you stuck your face out of a car driving a hundred miles per hour, your eyeballs would be sucked out of your head."

Sam thought for a second and then said, "Fake. If I stuck my head out a window of a car driving at a hundred miles an hour, my ears would come off first."

"Nope, eyes." Dottie opened hers wide and explained, "Eyes don't have much holding them in place."

"You two are such weirdos," a voice from behind them said.

Miles Huckatony.

For some reason, Miles Huckatony always walked close to

Dottie and Sam on the way to school. Miles Huckatony was in the same class as Sam and Dottie, and had been since first grade. He also lived somewhere close by. Dottie didn't know where. Actually, Dottie didn't want to know where. Miles had been a thorn in her side for years. That's how Ima put it after Dottie complained about Miles. "Miles Huckatony is a thorn in your side, but don't forget, Dottie, wherever there's a thorn, there's also a rose."

Dottie liked the part about the thorn. It sounded correct. The rose part, on the other hand, was a stretch.

Miles continued, "Your eyes can't be sucked out of your face, and neither can your ears. That's not possible."

Sam Batty and Dottie stopped talking. It wasn't that they minded him disagreeing with them. They were used to that. He always disagreed with them. Sam and Dottie stopped talking because Miles had a way of taking the fun out of everything, especially Truth or Fake. Dottie had tried many times to explain the game to Miles, but there was no point. Miles never understood why anyone would play a game that had no rules and didn't make any sense.

After a block, Sam leaned over and whispered, "You know, Dottie, now that I think about it, you're right. Eyes would be ripped out first and after that the ears and last to go would be the nose."

"Ohhh," Dottie sighed. "I forgot all about the nose." She took a second to picture a nose flying off a face. Dottie was so impressed by Sam Batty. No one else had a mind like his.

11. Are You Here?

Their teacher, Ms. Agna, was waiting by the door as they arrived. This was Ms. Agna's first year of teaching and Dottie thought very highly of her. She liked her manner, which was gentle. She liked her teaching, which used lots of paint and scissors, and she liked her smile, which felt like sunshine. She also liked how every day Ms. Agna greeted each student as they walked in.

Months ago, when school first started, Sam Batty told Dottie that Ms. Agna was exemplary.

"Exemplary," Dottie repeated. "Exemplary. Ex-emp-la-reee." She stretched out the word because it was so fun to say. "Ex-emp-la-reeee!" How could a word sound like a person? Dottie didn't have an answer to this question, but she knew it was true.

One of the things Dottie loved about the class was that everyone had a job. Jobs were fun because they didn't feel like school and every week their jobs changed. Last week Dottie was the door holder. Next week, she would be homework collector. This week, she was attendance helper.

Dottie grabbed the attendance sheet, went to the front of the class, and called out the names.

Her favorite part was when she got to her own name.

"Dottie Bing?" She paused and looked around. "Dottie Bing?" she repeated, this time sounding a little annoyed. "Dottie? Are you here? Is Dottie here?" And then she raised her hand up high and shouted, "Here I am! Right here!"

This made her topple over laughing. No one else seemed to think this was as funny as Dottie, but she didn't care.

As Ima once said, "Sometimes, all you've got is yourself." Dottie thought those were very wise words.

12. Is There a Problem?

Dottie was the first to admit that for all her years at Abrams Elementary School, lunch was a problem. To be more precise, the lunch monitor was the problem.

On the first day of every school year, Mr. Park introduced himself to the students. "My name is Mr. Park, but everyone calls me Mr. Shark because I never stop moving and I'm always watching you," he said. "Also, I can smell trouble from across the room. So, don't make trouble." As dangerous as a real shark might be, Mr. Shark was worse. Real sharks didn't have rules like Mr. Shark did. His favorite ones were: 1. Talk less, eat more. 2. No leaving your seat. 3. Take care of yourself, not others.

Every year Dottie hoped the rules would change. They never did.

Dottie and Sam plunked down in their normal seats.

"Truth or fake?" Sam asked, unzipping his lunch box. "If you swallow a piece of gum, it takes forty years to digest."

"That has to be true," Dottie said. She had no proof about this; she just liked the idea of it being true.

Sam nodded. "I swallowed gum yesterday."

"So, it won't be out of your stomach until you're—" Dottie added it up. "Fifty-one!"

"I'll be an old, old man," Sam said in a shaky voice.

They both giggled.

"Dottie! Sam!" Mr. Shark loomed over them. "Is there a problem?"

"No problem," they both said quickly.

"Then less talking, more eating!"

Truthfully, there *was* a problem. Sadly, there seemed to be no solution to the problem of Mr. Shark.

But it didn't matter. It was Friday. Dottie had two days away from Mr. Shark and even better, she had two days to build a tree house with Sam. Nothing was better than that.

13. Stranger than Brains?

After surviving lunch with Mr. Shark, the rest of the day was a piece of cake. That's what Ima always said when something went smoothly. And then she would ask why it wasn't a piece of pie. Ima loved pie the most. Once, she made Dottie a blueberry pie, but when the time came for them to eat it, she insisted they could not eat it using a fork. When Grandpa Walter caught them gobbling up blueberry pie with just their mouths, he shook his head and backed out of the room. Their faces stayed blue for a day.

On the walk home, Dottie and Sam talked only about the tree house, and when they arrived, they agreed to meet outside in ten minutes.

"HELLOOOOO!" Dottie shouted as she slammed the door shut.

She heard voices in the kitchen and headed that way.

But when she walked in, Grandpa Walter sat alone with

a book in his hand and the Chock full o'Nuts can beside him on the table. Next to the can were two mugs of coffee. Dottie knew it was coffee from the smell, but why were there two mugs when there was only one Grandpa Walter?

Dottie knew her mom was still at work. She peered around, hoping her dad was home with Jazzy. But there was no one but Grandpa Walter.

"Is Dad here?" Dottie asked.

Grandpa Walter said, "Collecting Jazzy."

Dottie didn't like that answer.

Grandpa Walter reached for one of the mugs of coffee but on the way to his mouth he missed and poured it all down his front. "Whoops!" Grandpa Walter stood up.

Dottie grabbed a dish towel for him.

Maybe that was why he had two cups? In case he spilled one? It was the only logical answer.

"Now let's see," Grandpa Walter said after he was done wiping up the mess. "Where was I?" He picked up the book and started to read.

Out loud.

To the can.

That was what Dottie had heard when she walked in. Grandpa Walter reading to the Chock full o'Nuts can, even though the can was just a can.

She felt her alligator squirming inside her belly. And this time it seemed to have brought a friend. Dottie frowned. A porcupine?

Ima had always loved being read to, even if it was Dottie doing the reading. Dottie listened to Grandpa Walter read. She didn't understand a word he was reading except that it was about someone named Miss Marple.

Grandpa Walter stopped mid-sentence. "Oh, Ima," he said. "I didn't see that coming. Did you?"

Without a thought, Dottie looked around, expecting to see Ima, expecting her to answer.

But Ima wasn't there. Of course she wasn't there. And she never would be. Not ever again.

"Truth or fake?" Dottie asked. Truth or Fake always took her mind off things she didn't want to think about—especially things like alligators and porcupines. Dottie repeated, "Truth or fake, a person can sneeze so hard, their brains come out their nose?"

Dottie had been saving this one up for a special occasion with Sam. She asked it because it was the first thing to pop into her head. Ima loved Truth or Fake, but Grandpa Walter called it hogwash. Right now, Dottie didn't mind if Grandpa Walter thought it was hogwash. She just wanted to stop thinking about Ima and for Grandpa Walter to stop thinking he was talking to Ima.

She waited for Grandpa Walter to say something. Anything. "Are you asking me if a person can sneeze so hard that their brains come out of their nose?"

Dottie nodded.

"Hmmm." Grandpa Walter frowned, deep in thought. At

last, he shrugged and said, "Stranger things have happened, so I'll say truth."

Dottie stood there in disbelief. Grandpa Walter had never once answered one of her Truth or Fake questions. And what did he even mean about stranger things happening? Before she could ask, Grandpa Walter yawned and stood up. "Time for our nap," he said, grabbing the can and leaving Dottie to wonder what could possibly be stranger than brains sneezing out of a nose.

Nothing came to her, but anything was better than thinking about Ima.

14. Do You Think That's a Good Idea?

Just after Grandpa Walter trudged upstairs, Dottie's mom, dad, and Jazzy arrived home.

Her mom and dad plunked down on the sofa exhausted from the week while Jazzy bounced into her favorite chair, flipped upside down, and hung there with her fingers touching the floor.

Besides cartwheeling, Jazzy loved hanging upside down. She could do it for hours.

"Have you seen Grandpa Walter?" Dottie's dad asked.

"Napping."

"That's good." Her dad nodded.

Dottie frowned. When was napping good? The answer was never. Just thinking about napping made Dottie squirmy all over. Luckily, the doorbell rang (Sam!), so she had something much better to think about (the tree house!).

"I'll be outside," Dottie announced.

Jazzy sat up. "Can I come with you?"

"No," Dottie answered fast.

"Why not?"

"Because," Dottie said, opening the door to Sam.

"Because why?" Jazzy yelled.

"Because—" Dottie paused trying to think of what to say. She knew she couldn't tell her that they were building a tree house and that Jazzy was not part of the tree house mission. Instead, she said, "Because Sam and I are busy." Dottie grabbed Sam. "Let's go, Sam."

Sam waved. "Hi, Mrs. Bing. Hi, Mr. Bing."

"Hi, Sam," Dottie's parents said.

"I can be busy too," Jazzy said, running after them. "Busy is easy."

"Dottie," her mom said. "Take Jazzy with you."

Dottie's heart fell and hit something spiky. (The porcupine?) "Please, Mom. Sam and I are doing something."

"Pleeease." Jazzy clasped her hands together and fell to her knees. "Please take me with you."

"What are you doing that Jazzy can't tag along with you?" Dottie's dad asked.

Technically, Dottie wasn't hiding the tree house from her parents. They were the kind of parents who believed kids could do things. Even slightly dangerous things. And, obviously, once the hammering started, everyone would know about the tree house. (There was no avoiding that.)

But for just a little while, she wanted it to be hers and

Sam's. She wanted the alligator (and now the porcupine) out of her and truly gone. Then she could include Jazzy.

"Dottie?" her dad said. "What's going on?"

"They're building a tree house," Jazzy said matter-of-factly. Dottie frowned. How did she know that?

Jazzy shrugged. "I found the picture."

This reminded Dottie of the time Grandpa Walter caught Ima sneaking a live chicken into the house as a surprise present. Ima had said, "Well, the cat is out of the bag." And then smiled and added, "Or in this case, a chicken is out of the bag."

Grandpa Walter loved the chicken and named her Feathers. Sadly, it turned out that Feathers was a rooster, not a hen, so Feathers found a new home at Happy Dirt Farm. Ima and Grandpa Walter visited him regularly. At least until Ima couldn't visit anymore.

Now the tree house was out of the bag, and it was Dottie's fault for forgetting to hide the picture.

"You're building a tree house?" her dad asked, surprise written all across his face. "And you weren't going to tell us?"

Dottie nodded as Sam stood sheepishly next to her.

"That's wonderful," Dottie's mom said.

"I like your initiative," Dottie's dad added.

"I love tree houses," Jazzy announced for no reason at all. "I've never been in one. Maybe I will hate it. Do you think I will hate it? I hope I don't hate it. Could you make a small tree house? The one you drew looks very tall."

Before Dottie could answer any of these questions, her dad asked, "Which tree?"

"The one on the side of the house," Dottie said.

"The one by your window?" her mom asked.

Dottie and Sam nodded.

"And you're starting now?" her dad asked.

Dottie and Sam nodded.

"Do you think that's a good idea?" Dottie's dad asked.

Dottie hated questions like this. They always felt like a trick. First off because these were the kind of questions where the person asking obviously already had an answer in mind. And second off because the answer was obviously not the same as Dottie's.

Before Dottie answered her dad, he said, "I don't mean you can't build the tree house. I mean Grandpa Walter is napping and this might not be the best time to build the tree house."

"Oh," Dottie said, relieved. "We'll be quiet. Really quiet."

"I don't think that will work," Dottie's mom said.

"We'll be really, really quiet," Dottie said hopefully.

Dottie's dad shook his head. "Just wait until your grandpa wakes up. I'm sure he won't nap for long."

If Dottie's past experience was anything to go by, then it was clear her dad had no idea how long 'not long' was to Grandpa Walter.

"What if we don't bang at all?" Dottie asked.

"Dottie," her dad said. This time meaning it.

"Okay, okay." Dottie knew when she was beat.

45

"Jazzy?" Her mom asked. "Do you want to go with them?"

Jazzy shook her head. "Not if they aren't doing anything." She returned to hanging upside down from her chair as Dottie and Sam walked outside to wait for Grandpa Walter to wake up.

"How long do you think he'll sleep for?" Sam asked.

Sadly, Dottie had no answer for that question.

15. What's Scavenging?

Dottie and Sam dropped down onto the grass.

"What are we going to do until Grandpa Walter wakes up?" Dottie asked, pulling at the grass.

It was very exasperating. *Exasperating* was Sam's word for being mad. It was impossible to spell but so fun to say. The exasperation filled Dottie up like drinking too much fizzy water (or having an alligator and his best friend the porcupine curled up in her belly). Either way, she did not have room for all these feelings. She just wanted to build the tree house. She *had* to build the tree house.

Dottie pulled at the grass again. "Do you think it's strange that Grandpa Walter showed up the very day we were beginning this?"

Sam shrugged. "Stranger things have happened."

"Like what?" Dottie asked, shocked.

Sam looked down. "My mom didn't think she'd ever have another baby and now look."

Dottie bit her lip. "You know, it's going to be okay. Jazzy isn't that bad."

Sam nodded, but Dottie could tell he didn't mean it. She could also tell he needed the conversation changed. "Do you think there's anything stranger than brains coming out of a nose?"

Sam Batty shook his head. "No."

"That's what I thought," Dottie said. "Grandpa Walter disagrees."

"You asked him?"

Dottie shrugged. "I needed to change the subject."

Sam thought and then said, "He does keep your grandma in a Chock full o'Nuts can. That's pretty strange."

"It was their favorite brand of coffee," Dottie reminded Sam.

"It's still strange," Sam said.

"Is it stranger than being in a coffin?" Dottie asked.

"It's definitely more unusual," Sam said.

Dottie wondered if unusual and strange were the same thing.

Before she figured out the answer to this, Sam sat straight up. "What have we been thinking?"

Dottie listed their thoughts on her fingers. "That we want to build the tree house. That we can't because Grandpa Walter is napping. That your mom having a baby is stranger than Grandpa Walter arriving on the day we want to build a tree house, and that there is something stranger than brains coming out of a nose. Am I forgetting anything?"

"No. No. No, not that. I mean thinking that we could build the tree house if he wasn't napping."

"What do you mean?" Dottie asked.

"We don't have anything to build it with!"

Dottie gasped. Sam was completely correct. How could she have missed that?

Sam and Dottie ran back into the house, snuck through quietly, grabbed their drawing, and slipped out again without being seen.

"Mostly we need wood," Sam said, studying it.

"A lot of wood," Dottie added.

"I guess some rope would be good," Sam said. "Maybe some rocks."

"What do we need rocks for?" Dottie asked.

"I don't know, but if we find some, I'm sure we could use them."

They started off by rummaging in their own homes. In Sam's basement they found old clothes, toys, and a broken scooter. In Dottie's they found a bunch of cardboard, some garden tools, and a dead mouse. But no wood.

"I thought for sure we would have some," Dottie said.

"Me too." Sam sighed.

"What do we do now?" Dottie asked.

Sam tapped his forehead, which was what he did when he was deep in thought. "We need to forage," he finally said.

"What's foraging?" Dottie asked.

"It's scavenging."

"What's scavenging?"

"It's searching," Sam explained. "We need to search the neighborhood. See if anyone left anything out."

Foraging and scavenging sounded like a treasure hunt. Dottie knew about treasure hunts thanks to Ima. Ima loved treasure hunts. She would spend days thinking up clues, then leave them out for Dottie to follow, one clue leading to the next until it brought Dottie to the final treasure. Her favorite treasure was a tea party Ima organized. And then there was the time Dottie made a treasure hunt for Ima. The treasure was a blanket fort with a pile of books and pillows inside.

Dottie's stomach churned as the alligator and porcupine stomped around, making a fuss. Dottie closed her eyes, remembering Ima and the fort. That was the same day Ima had told her about wanting a tree house.

The tree house. Just thinking about the tree house calmed Dottie. Her belly settled. She could breathe again. Dottie opened her eyes to Sam's face smiling at her. Waiting for her answer.

"What do you think?" Sam asked.

"I think you are brilliant," Dottie said. (Sam's word for smart.) Dottie thought she was pretty brilliant too. The tree house was definitely the answer to her problem. Now all she needed to do was build it. And everyone knew that was the best part of a tree house.

16. Do You See What I See?

After explaining their plans to their parents, Sam and Dottie grabbed the red wagon sometimes used to pull Jazzy around in and got under way.

They started by going around their block. In front of the house with the loud dog, they found some rope and a few bricks. At Mr. Bombachi's, who lived on the corner, they found an old lawn mower he wanted to get rid of.

As good as the lawn mower was, they couldn't think how they'd use it, so they left it behind. Still, no wood.

Next, they walked three blocks over toward Beecher Street, where someone was giving away a potty seat (which they did not want) and a pair of broken roller skates (which they left for someone else to have). They cut through the alley connecting Thirty-eighth and Thirty-ninth Streets. There were a lot of trash cans but nothing else.

It seemed like they had been walking forever when Sam said, "This isn't going as well as I hoped."

Dottie agreed.

"Can we build a tree house without wood?" Sam said.

Dottie didn't think so. What would they do if they didn't find any? If Ima were here, she would know what to do. Ima always knew what to do. Like the time the toilet clogged and was about to overflow all over the floor and Grandpa Walter ran out and Ima walked in, turned one knob, and stopped the whole disaster. Without Ima, that would have been a remarkably different memory. Dottie didn't know what to do, but she knew that she would not give up.

"We just have to keep looking."

Sam nodded. "Okay, let's keep looking."

Dottie and Sam wound their way along, hoping with every house they passed that they might find wood. They turned this way and that until coming upon a street Dottie had never walked down. The houses were larger with tall shrubs in front of them. A feeling of hopelessness washed over Dottie as she and Sam marched along. She was trying to stay positive, but not even Dottie was silly enough to believe that anyone on a street like this would leave wood just sitting out waiting for two kids who needed to build a tree house.

She felt something deep in her gut squeeze tight. She froze. This wasn't just the alligator or even the alligator *and* the porcupine. There was a new animal, and from the squeezing of her guts, it had to be an octopus. Nothing else could squeeze so tightly.

Dottie stopped walking. "We'll never find anything. Let's just go home."

"I'm not letting you give up," Sam said. He grabbed her arm and pulled. "We have to keep looking."

"What's the point?" Dottie whined. The octopus was crushing all the hope out of her.

Sam came around from behind and pushed her forward. "Come on, Dottie. Please? I need this tree house too. Pretty soon there'll be a crying baby in my life, and I'll want a place to escape!"

"Okay," she said. The search still felt futile (Sam's word for hopeless). But Dottie could look a little longer for Sam. She'd do anything for him. But because it was difficult to move with three animals tightly wedged inside her, she let Sam push her down the road, walking past house after house and still finding nothing. (At least they had each other.)

There was only one last house on the block. A towering shrub planted next to the house blocked their view. Neither could see what was on the other side.

Dottie took a deep breath. "This is it."

"This is it," Sam agreed.

"If there's nothing here, we give up."

"For today," Sam added.

"For today." Dottie nodded.

They walked slowly, like their feet were scared of what they wouldn't find. Dottie closed her eyes and held on to the corner of Sam's shirt. She couldn't look. It was too hard.

Then Sam stopped. "Do you see what I see?" he asked.

"No." Dottie shook her head. Her eyes were still closed.

"Open your eyes," Sam ordered.

Right there, on an overgrown lawn, lay a huge pile of wood, and leaning beside it there was a sign that read: *FREE WOOD*.

With this wood, a tree house could be built. Dottie could picture it all. It was going to be amazing. It was going to be incredible. It was going to be majestic.

"It'll take us at least three trips to get all this," Dottie said as she and Sam tossed some into the wagon.

"Maybe even four!" Sam beamed.

They were about to leave with the first load when a voice behind them said, "What are you weirdos doing?"

Miles Huckatony.

17. Where Do You Want All of This?

Dottie's first question was how could she get as far away from Miles as possible?

Her second question was how could she get as far away as possible without speaking to him?

Her third question was what was *he* doing here anyway?

The first two questions were answered quickly by Sam, who instead of bounding down the street like Dottie was thinking about, waved to Miles and said, "Hey." Then he elbowed Dottie, who grudgingly mumbled, "Hey Miles."

Miles nodded at them and asked, "So, what are you doing?"

The last thing Dottie wanted was to tell Miles anything. Dottie knew that he would manage to take all the fun out of it, like always. During PE, Miles turned everything into a winning/losing game. During art, he had the habit of swinging paintbrushes around like they were swords and challenging students to a duel, which only led to paint flying about over everything and everyone. And then, there was the long history with Truth or Fake, which proved without a doubt that Miles was incapable of experiencing joy.

"Well," Miles said again. "Are you going to answer my question?"

Dottie shrugged. "Why do you want to know?"

"Because I live here," Miles said.

"You live *here*?" Dottie gulped. If she had known that, she wouldn't have stopped for the wood. (But at least now her third question was answered.)

Sam said, "Your family is getting rid of a lot of wood."

"What's it to you?" Miles asked.

"Nothing," Dottie said. Why did Miles have to be so argumentative? (And yes, Dottie learned that word from Sam.)

Dottie grabbed the wagon handle. "Thanks for the wood," she said, and started off. She did not have to put up with Miles. Sam followed.

"Are you going to tell me what you're doing with it all?" Miles shouted after Dottie.

Evasive was the word Sam used when he and Dottie wanted to avoid anyone knowing what they were up to. And evasive was what Dottie wanted to be now. Before she could even attempt it, Miles said, "I'll get my wheelbarrow and help you."

Dottie and Sam each took a step backward.

"It's obvious you need more than one wagon load," Miles said.

How was it obvious? Dottie wanted to ask, but he ran away

before she could
and, by the time he
came back pulling a wheelbarrow, she had forgotten.

Dottie and Sam watched as Miles
filled his wheelbarrow and then headed up
the street in the direction of Dottie's and Sam's
houses. Miles looked behind him. "Are you two
coming or what?"

Dottie and Sam followed Miles. As they walked along
Dottie realized they were closer to her house than she thought.

She and Sam must have been wandering in circles for hours.

When they reached Dottie's house, Miles stopped. "Where do you want all this?"

Dottie pointed to the side of the house.

"Over there?" Miles asked. "By the tree?"

Dottie nodded.

Miles Huckatony wheeled over to the tree with Sam and Dottie behind him.

"Are you building a tree house?" Miles asked.

Dottie couldn't avoid telling him any longer. (Especially after he lugged all that wood for them.) "Eventually," she said. Just because she felt she needed to answer didn't mean she needed to answer him in detail.

Miles nodded like he understood. "Should we go back for the rest?"

"Yeah," Sam said.

As they walked past Zombie House, Miles paused. "What's the deal with that house? It's a mess."

"Zombies live there," Dottie said, before she remembered that Miles had no imagination.

"Zombies don't exist," he said.

Dottie didn't argue. What would have been the point? Although she did notice that as they passed Zombie House, Miles picked up his step. Maybe Miles did have an imagination. Maybe. But Dottie doubted it.

Miles helped Dottie and Sam bring three more loads of wood—which was all the wood—to the tree.

"Hey Miles," Sam said, after the last load was dumped. "Thanks for your help."

"Whatever," Miles said, walking away. He didn't take his eyes off Zombie House until he was at the end of the block and then he ran as if his life depended on it.

Sam and Dottie stood in silence, watching as he disappeared down the road.

Sam turned to Dottie. "Miles Huckatony helped us. Miles Huckatony doesn't help anyone."

Dottie nodded. "I think we discovered what is stranger than brains coming out of a nose."

"I think we did," Sam agreed, just as his mom called his cell and told him to come home.

18. Who's Lucky?

Phenomenal," Dottie said when she woke up the next day.

Phenomenal was Sam's word for anything better than amazing. There were many reasons why this word was perfect for today.

One reason was that weekends were phenomenal. (And Saturdays were especially phenomenal because there was still another day to the weekend once this day was over.)

Another reason was because Dottie had picked the bottom bunk last night, which meant that after Jazzy slipped into the bed and pushed her out, she didn't have far to fall.

But, the biggest phenomenal reason of all was the tree house she and Sam were building today. It was so phenomenal that Dottie didn't even mind MacFurry using her foot as a scratching post or that she had to muddle through a half an hour until she and Sam met.

Grandpa Walter was playing cards with the Chock full

o'Nuts can when Dottie walked into the kitchen. There were, as usual, two cups of coffee sitting on the counter, but it was the card game that tied Dottie's mind into knots. Or maybe it was the octopus.

"Morning Dottie," Grandpa Walter said as he laid down a card. Dottie knew without asking that he was playing rummy. It was Ima's favorite and Dottie and Ima used to play it all the time. There was a pickup pile facing down and a discard pile facing up, but who was he playing against?

Dottie watched Grandpa Walter pick up some cards next to the Chock full o'Nuts can.

Oh no. No. No. No. She thought, *Please don't tell me he's playing cards with Ima.*

Grandpa Walter picked a card from the pile, examined it, and then laughed. "Oh," he exclaimed. "Aren't you lucky?"

"Who's lucky?" Dottie asked, even though she knew the answer, and, for some reason, the answer bothered her.

"Ima, naturally."

"Ima," she repeated. She had been right.

Grandpa Walter laid down four cards with the number nine and another three cards that were all queens. "And she wins again," Grandpa Walter announced.

"Again?" Dottie asked.

Grandpa Walter smiled. "She always wins."

How could Grandpa Walter lose to someone who wasn't even there? And on top of that, he actually looked happy. Dottie shook her head. It was silly to think she could ever understand

Grandpa Walter. Besides, Dottie had her own problems—like pushing away the alligator, porcupine, and octopus who were determined to grab her attention.

Dottie looked at the clock; there were still fifteen minutes to go before Sam met her, but Dottie couldn't stay here a second longer. She left to wait for Sam outside.

Everything would be better with Sam.

Unfortunately, the scowl on Sam's face when he walked up the driveway told Dottie this was not the case. A scowl was like a frown but worse (at least that's how Sam described it).

And after Sam explained about the surprise visit to Aunt Sylvie's, she understood why.

"For the whole weekend?" Dottie asked.

Sam nodded. "Last family trip as the three of us."

Dottie pretended to be okay and told Sam to have a good time. "In fact," she added, "don't have a good time, have a great time!" And she meant it. She hated seeing Sam sad. And even though it was a struggle to get the words out, she made sure to say, "Don't worry about me. The tree house can wait."

Sam's mom called from the driveway. "Time to go, Sam!"

Sam smiled at Dottie. "We'll start on Monday," he reassured her. "Right after school. Nothing will stop us," he shouted as he climbed into his car.

Dottie stood there, watching the car disappear around the corner. If only Dottie were as lucky as Ima, Sam wouldn't be gone, the tree house wouldn't have to wait, and an alligator, a porcupine, and an octopus wouldn't be biting, needling, and squishing her. But no one was as lucky as Ima. That was clear when she walked back into the kitchen and found Grandpa Walter still playing cards against her and still losing.

Dottie sank into a chair resigned to the fact that this weekend had gone from phenomenal to miserable. (And there was nothing she could do about it.)

19. Why Did You Say That?

Two days later, Dottie woke up smooshed. On one side was the wall. On the other side was Jazzy and on the bottom was MacFurry, happily gnawing on her toes. But none of this mattered to Dottie. What was important was that Dottie had survived the weekend. It was Monday! Monday! Monday! Monday! Sam was home and after school, they could start the tree house.

Finally.

The day couldn't get better than it already was. Or so she thought, until she slipped into the bathroom seconds before Grandpa Walter.

"I won't be long," she shouted through the door. And in her case, not long was really not long.

As Dottie skipped downstairs, dressed and ready for the day, it felt like her life was turning a corner. That's what Ima said when she was halfway through something challenging like a crossword puzzle or a long book or scrubbing the bathtub. Dottie could hear her clearly. "Looks like I've really turned a corner, Dot." And then she'd get back to it because turning a corner wasn't the same as being done.

And because she got into the bathroom first, Grandpa Walter was not yet in the kitchen drinking coffee or playing cards with the Chock full o'Nuts can. On top of that, there was no sign of the alligator, porcupine, or octopus. Now, this was the way life was supposed to be!

She gobbled up breakfast, grabbed her backpack, and was out the door with an overflowing sense of optimism. Everything was going to work out.

When Dottie met up with Sam, he briefly told her about Aunt Sylvie and how they went to a waterpark all together, but then they switched to more important topics (the tree house). They were almost at school when Miles Huckatony walked up behind them and barged in between them.

"What happened?" he demanded. "You haven't even started the tree house!"

He sounded as annoyed about this as she was, which irritated Dottie since the tree house had nothing to do with him. Then she wondered how he even knew they hadn't worked on it and as if he heard her question he said, "I walked by your house on Sunday. You haven't done a thing. And you probably never will. Will you?" Miles didn't wait for an answer. "Then all that wood will go to waste."

Although Dottie's rule was to always ignore Miles, this

morning she felt intrepid. *Intrepid* was Sam's word for brave or fearless. "Not that it is any of your business," she said. "But we begin today. Right after school."

"I'll believe it when I see it," Miles said.

"If you don't believe it, come and see it for yourself." Wow, she really *was* feeling intrepid.

"I will," Miles said, nodding emphatically, and then running off ahead of Dottie and Sam to line up for school.

Dottie would show Miles Huckatony what good tree house builders they were. She turned to Sam, expecting him to feel as intrepid as she was, but he was frowning. "Why did you say that?" Sam asked.

Dottie gulped. Why had she said that? At the time, it seemed like a good idea, but now that she thought about it, she realized what a terrible idea it was.

Sam stared at her, waiting for an answer to his question about why she did it. She knew she didn't have a good answer and she also knew that when faced with a question too hard to answer, there was only one choice: Change the topic.

"Truth or fake?" Dottie asked. "If you drank a hundred gallons of milk it would leak out through your skin."

Right away, Sam started to argue about how if that was true, what else could leak out of their bodies? Food? Guts? Blood?

Imagining food soaking through their skin got them laughing so hard that by the time they lined up, Miles Huckatony was the furthest thing from their minds.

20. He's What?

Besides the small hiccup with Miles, the rest of the day continued to be good.

In class, they started a new unit on insects. Ms. Agna drew names from a hat to decide the bug each student would study. Dottie got the dung beetle, which made her extremely pleased. Then, at lunch, it turned out Mr. Shark was out of school, and they had a substitute (anyone was better than Mr. Shark). And Miles didn't appear once on the walk home, which gave Dottie hope that maybe he wouldn't show up at her house.

When Sam and Dottie parted ways, agreeing to meet up in half an hour, Dottie trotted into her house.

Dottie found her mom and dad whispering in the kitchen. Her dad being home wasn't a surprise. He was always home on Mondays, but her mom never was.

They looked up when she walked in and immediately stopped talking.

"What's wrong?" Dottie asked. She knew trouble when she saw it.

"Dottie," her mom said, and tapped a chair beside her. "Come sit down. We need to talk."

Dottie did what she was asked, but she didn't like it.

"We need to talk about Grandpa Walter," her mom said.

"We're worried about him." Her dad frowned.

"What's there to worry about?" Dottie asked. Sure, he played cards with the can and talked to it and read to it, but other than that he seemed fine. In fact, better than fine. He seemed genuinely happy.

Dottie's mom said, "We don't think he should be alone."

Dottie was confused.

Dottie's dad said, "He's sad."

"Sad?" Dottie asked. If anyone was sad, it was her. In fact, she was the one building a whole entire tree house to get rid of her sadness. Grandpa Walter was the one smiling.

Her mom took Dottie's hand. "We've asked him to stay a little longer."

"Stay?" Dottie pulled her hand back. "Here?"

Dottie's mom nodded.

Dottie's dad said, "Since Ima died, he's not the same."

Not the same as what? Dottie wondered.

"I don't like him living alone," her dad added.

The animals in Dottie's stomach churned.

"We know this is a big ask," her dad said. "But he needs to stay with us."

"For how long?" Dottie managed to squeak.

"It won't be long," her dad said. "Just until he's happy."

Happy? Dottie thought. He seemed happy to Dottie. How much happier did they want him to get?

Her mom said, "He won't stay unless you agree. He knows he's in your room."

Dottie's brain froze. Should she let Grandpa Walter stay?

That question was too hard to answer because really her answer was no. Having him around was tough. Not only because he slept in her room and was interfering with her building the tree house, but for some other reason, one that she couldn't put her finger on.

Her mom and dad waited.

There must be a different question that would be easier to answer. Dottie thought and thought and then it hit her. What if the question wasn't should she let Grandpa Walter stay? What if the question was: What would Ima do? That was easy. Ima would let Grandpa Walter stay. Dottie didn't like it, but it was an answer. "He can stay," Dottie said.

Dottie's mom and dad hugged her.

"But I can still build the tree house, right?"

Dottie's parents exchanged looks, then her dad said, "Let's hold off on the tree house, while he's here. The noise might bother him."

It was a mystery to Dottie how her parents were so sure about what bothered Grandpa Walter and, at the same time, were so oblivious to what bothered Dottie. (*Oblivious* was

Sam's fancier and much more fun way to say they didn't notice it at all.)

What wasn't a mystery was how in a few short days her world turned upside down and there was nothing she could do to stop it.

21. How Do We Know When He's Happy?

After the meeting with her parents, Dottie needed some fresh air. She hoped that going outside would quiet the cacophony in her head. *Cacophony* was how Sam described sounds that were loud and yucky. This was different from sounds that were loud and fun like the ones on a playground. Sadly, Sam never told her a word for that kind of sound. (She'd have to ask.)

Outside on the front lawn, Dottie plunked down and stared across the street at Zombie House.

She let her eyes go all squinty and blurry. Weird things always happened when she did this. Sometimes, she even saw things move inside the house.

Like right then. A shadow passed. A curtain fluttered.

It gave her the shivers and scared the guts out of her, but in a really good way. In a way that took her mind off everything else.

She was still riveted to Zombie House when Sam appeared next to her. "I told my parents I would be busy all afternoon. It's just you, me, and the tree house."

Dottie's face scrunched up. The mesmerizing (another of Sam's words) power of Zombie House snapped, and Dottie turned to Sam. "We've got a problem."

"We can't build the tree house," Sam said knowingly.

Dottie gaped at him, confused how he knew.

"What other problem could it be?"

"Grandpa Walter is staying."

"For how long?" Sam sounded as disappointed as Dottie felt.

"Until he's happy," Dottie said.

"How do we know when he's happy?"

Dottie sighed. "I didn't even know he was so sad, so your guess is as good as mine."

From down the block they could see Miles heading their way. He was on a bike and raced toward them, turning at the last minute to stop. "How's the tree house?" Miles didn't wait for an answer. "I knew you wouldn't do it," he said.

"You don't know anything," Dottie said, feeling especially grumpy. She just wanted him to go away and there was only one way to get Miles Huckatony to do that.

"Truth or fake?" she asked Sam. "Blood is red because we eat tomatoes."

"What?" Miles grouched.

"That's an interesting question," Sam said, catching on right away to Dottie's plan. "I think it's true. What else could make blood red?"

"You have got to be kidding!" Miles hit his head with his hand. "It's fake! Fake! Fake! Fake!"

"I guess it could be red from eating strawberries," Dottie said, ignoring Miles completely.

"Or beets," Sam added.

"Or red cabbage," Dottie suggested.

"You cannot be serious! My dad is a doctor! Blood is not red because you eat tomatoes! I can't believe you two." He rolled his eyes and biked away.

Sam turned back to Dottie. "Let's hope making Grandpa Walter happy is as easy as annoying Miles."

Dottie hoped so too. She really didn't know how long she could last without the tree house.

22. Which Was He?

The next morning, Dottie woke with Jazzy spread out on top of her like jam on toast. Dottie stayed put, instead of wriggling away. All her dreams of building a tree house had melted, leaving a puddle and not much else. Without the tree house, why get out of bed?

Then MacFurry bit her, and even though she was wearing socks, Dottie found a compelling (and painful) answer to *that* question.

Dottie huffed around. Who cared if she was late for school? Who cared that the bathroom was empty? Who cared that Grandpa Walter was downstairs sitting at the table with the Chock full o'Nuts can and two mugs of coffee? Except suddenly, Dottie did care. In fact, it really bugged her. "Grandpa Walter? Why do you need two cups of coffee?"

Grandpa Walter smiled. "One for me and one for Ima."

"Oh," Dottie said, about to ask him how Ima would drink

it, but then he opened the newspaper to the funnies, reading them out loud and giggling over them like Ima was actually in the room.

Dottie stomped away. How could her parents think he was sad when he could laugh at the funnies?

She really wanted to know the answer. Which was he? Happy or sad? She would have asked him right there and then, but the words stuck in her throat and there was no getting them out. Not with an alligator, a porcupine, an octopus, and now a kangaroo clogging it all up.

23. What Was She Doing Wrong?

When Dottie got home from school she was in as bad a mood as when she left, but Sam insisted that she come outside as soon as she could. "It's not good to be cooped up in your house," he argued.

Dottie shrugged. "Inside or outside. What's the difference?"

"How's Grandpa Walter?"

Dottie shrugged. She didn't have words for how sad she felt, but the pain in her stomach said it all.

"I'm sorry," Sam said. "But we'll figure it out. Remember, we didn't think we'd find the wood and we did that."

Dottie could always count on Sam to stay positive.

"In times like this, Dottie, there is only one thing to do."

"Change the subject," Dottie said, finishing Sam's thought.

Sam nodded. "Truth or fake? If we walked into Zombie House, we would survive."

"Definitely fake," Dottie said. "We'd get pulled in and eaten alive in two seconds flat."

Sam pretended to be a zombie about to eat Dottie and Dottie pretended to be one about to eat him. They both cracked up.

"Hey, weirdos," Miles Huckatony said, riding up on his bike.

Sam and Dottie stopped pretending to be zombies.

"What are you doing?" Miles asked.

Dottie found it baffling that Miles kept wanting to know what they were doing. *Baffling* was a better word than *confusing*, and Dottie was forever grateful to Sam for introducing it to her. Miles clearly didn't like Dottie and Sam, so why did he never leave them alone?

Ima always said, "Everyone fails, but champions never give up."

Dottie wasn't sure why she thought of this right now and she wasn't sure what it had to do with Miles, and she knew for sure that she was not a champion because she had not been able to build the tree house, but there was something inside her. Maybe it was the alligator, or the porcupine, maybe it was the octopus or the kangaroo, whatever it was, it made her want to face Miles and not simply by annoying him with Truth or Fake.

Today, she wanted to get rid of him for good. (Today, she would be a champion.)

24. You Think You Can Handle the Truth?

Are you sure you want to know what we're doing?" Dottie asked Miles.

Miles Huckatony leaned on the handlebars of his bike. "Why wouldn't I?"

Dottie said, "You think you can handle the truth?"

"The truth?" Miles asked.

Sam repeated, "The truth."

"I can handle it," Miles said. "I can handle it just fine."

Dottie pointed across the street. "We were talking about that house over there."

"Zombie House? Yeah, you told me, and I don't believe you. My dad says it's just an old, empty, run-down house that no one wants."

"Looks can be deceiving," Sam said.

"Have you ever been inside?" Miles asked.

"Inside?" Sam Batty scoffed. "And be turned into zombies? No way."

"But," Dottie said. "Because you don't believe in zombies, you could go in there."

"Go in an old house?" Miles shrugged. "Sure, I could. But why would I?"

Dottie raised her eyebrows. She knew the door was locked and they'd never get in, but she had another idea. "I heard a story about kids who just knocked on the front door and were never heard from again."

"Knocked on the door?" Miles pulled a face. "I don't buy it."

Sam nodded. "I know that story too. They up and disappeared. I hear they might have been turned into zombies."

"You can't turn into a zombie from touching a door," Miles said dismissively.

And then Dottie said, "You want to test it and see?"

Miles stared at the house. "Knock on the door? Of Zombie House?"

Dottie nodded. "Unless you're too scared?"

"Scared?" Miles repeated. "I'm not scared of anything."

And, to Dottie's amazement, he hopped off his bike. She didn't think Miles was capable of fun. But this was fun.

Sam smiled. "We all run over and touch the door. On the count of three. One. Two. Three." And they all sprang into action. The three of them ran across the street, past the tree and across the Zombie Yard. They ran up to the Zombie Door. Dottie was in the lead. As she reached her hand out, for one iota, she wondered if touching the door might change her forever, but Sam and Miles were right behind her. She wasn't going to let Miles get to it first. She slapped the door hard.

A split second later, Sam and then Miles did the same.

The three of them ran back as fast as their legs would move, and maybe even screamed . . . probably screamed . . . definitely screamed until they were safe in Dottie's yard, where they collapsed onto the grass.

"We're alive," Miles exclaimed.

"Did you think we wouldn't be?" Sam asked.

"I knew I'd be okay," Miles said, laughing. "I wasn't sure about you two."

Dottie lay there very still and quiet and then suddenly a strange gurgling, choking sound bubbled out of her. "KUH-GH-GHH!KHHHHH."

The hand that had touched the door slowly curled up into a claw. It reached up toward the sky and then over Dottie's head, moving slowly toward her neck. Dottie tried to speak but only the choking sound came out. "KUHGH-GHH!"

"Dottie," Sam Batty said. "Stop it."

"We know you're faking!" Miles said.

"KUHGH-GHH!" The sounds kept churning. And as if it was moving with a mind of its own, the hand inched closer and closer to Dottie's neck. "NO!" Dottie screamed through the gurgles.

Her other hand grabbed hold of the curled one, trying to keep it away. "NO!" She struggled. "NO!"

Sam Batty and Miles sat up.

"Dottie?" Sam Batty said. "What's going on?"

"Is she okay?" Miles sounded worried.

"KUH-GH-GHH!" The gurgling noise didn't stop. Dottie's curled hand clasped around her neck.

Miles and Sam jumped up.

"Dottie!" Sam hollered. "Stop messing around!"

"I'm getting out of here!" Miles screamed, and started for his bike.

And that's when Dottie couldn't hold her laughter in anymore. It shook her whole body and she had to take gulps of air before she could finally speak again. "You should see the look on your faces!"

Miles threw down his bike. "I knew you were faking," he said.

Dottie couldn't stop laughing. "That was majestic," she said.

"I don't think that's how to use that word," Miles said.

"I think it is," Dottie said.

Sam started to laugh. "I wouldn't argue with her if I were you. It's a losing battle. But Dottie, if you ever do that again, I will tergiversate you."

"Tergiversate?" Miles asked. "*That's* not a real word."

"It is," Sam said.

"Do you know what it means?" Miles asked Dottie.

"No idea," Dottie said. "But whatever it is, it doesn't sound good."

"It isn't," Sam said. "So be careful."

Miles sat back down with Dottie and Sam. "That was fun," Miles said.

"It was," Sam said.

"Yup," Dottie agreed. And she realized that as much as she hated Miles, the truth was that maybe he wasn't as bad as she'd thought.

25. Different How?

"So, why haven't you started the tree house?" Miles asked.

All of a sudden, Dottie was brought back to reality, which included four animals pounding away at her insides and the fact that Miles was Miles and just because they had a little fun didn't mean Dottie trusted him.

"Look," Miles said. "I know I can be a jerk, but things are different."

"Different how?" Dottie asked.

Miles shrugged. "The zombies brought us together."

Dottie was surprised he said this, considering he didn't even believe in zombies.

Sam shrugged. "I think he's right."

Hmmm. Dottie thought about it. If Sam agreed with him, then maybe she should too.

"I mean it," Miles said.

Dottie nodded. The zombies had brought them together.

So, she told Miles about how Grandpa Walter arrived out of the blue and how because the tree was right outside Dottie's window where Grandpa Walter was staying they weren't allowed to bother him. She left out the part about Ima, the Chock full o'Nuts can, and the sadness. (She didn't know him well enough for *that*.)

"So how long will he stay?" Miles asked.

Sam shook his head. "We don't know."

They were all quiet for a while.

Miles said, "Would it bother him if you built it here?"

"Here?" Sam asked.

"Yeah," Miles said.

"You mean, in front of her house?" Sam asked.

"Yeah." Miles nodded.

"Why would we build a tree house here?" Dottie asked. "There isn't a tree."

"It's far away from his window, so the noise wouldn't bother him." Miles shrugged. "I mean, it's a way to start on the tree house."

Dottie was not convinced that building the tree house on the ground would make her happy.

Miles said, "Then when your grandpa leaves, you could move it and finish it in the tree."

Dottie and Sam looked at each other and then Sam said, "Truth or fake? Miles Huckatony is a genius."

Miles kicked the grass. "You know I hate that game."

"But you *are* a genius," Dottie said. "Sam is right." Additionally, Ima had been right too. Miles wasn't only a thorn in Dottie's side. He was also a rose. And if that could be true, then honestly anything was possible. (Including building a tree house.)

"Well? What are you standing around for?" Miles asked. "We haven't got all day!"

Dottie jumped to it, happy that Miles was as excited as she and Sam to build the tree house, and also happy that Miles could still be a thorn in her side. (Too much change all at once was hard to handle.)

26. Maybe a Million?

Dottie ran inside her home, returning a few minutes later with three hammers and a box of nails. While she was gone, Sam and Miles had dragged as much wood as they could around to the front lawn.

"Where do we begin?" Miles asked. He wasn't as bossy as Dottie thought he would be.

"The platform," she said.

"Cool," Miles said. "How do we do that?"

Sam and Dottie laid the boards out so they were side by side.

"And now," Sam said, "we crisscross another layer on top and then nail them to the bottom."

Miles nodded. "Sort of like in art class when we did the weaving project." Miles paused and added, "I hated that project."

"We need to hammer these together," Dottie said, ignoring Miles. Her hands were trembly and her insides felt like fizzy water. She paused, wondering which animal it was this time, but she realized the answer was no animal. This feeling was excitement and joy. The tree house really was going to change everything.

"It needs to be bigger," Sam said.

"Yeah," Miles said. "Way bigger."

They were piling more wood out on the ground when Jazzy walked outside.

Jazzy squinted up at Miles and then said, "Are you Miles?" Miles nodded.

"I've heard about you," Jazzy said. "And none of it is good."

Dottie made a face. She felt a little bad, but just for getting caught.

Miles shrugged. "Yeah. My mom says I have big feelings."

That was a nice way to describe it. Ima would have liked that. And now that Dottie thought about it, she had to admit that she had big feelings too. Wasn't that why she was building the tree house in the first place? And she knew Sam had big feelings about the new baby. That's why he needed the tree house.

"Who are you?" Miles asked, interrupting Dottie's thinking.

"I'm her sister." She pointed at Dottie. "Jazzy."

"You look like sisters," Miles said, nodding. Then he went back to overlapping the wood so they could hammer the boards

together. Dottie grabbed a nail, pointed it down, and was about to hammer when Jazzy said, "What are you making?"

Dottie stopped, hammer in midair. "The floor," she said, lining up the hammer and nail again.

"The floor of what?" Jazzy asked.

Dottie's hammer stopped. She needed to concentrate, or she would bang her finger. "The tree house," she said, getting the hammer ready.

"Can I help?" Jazzy said.

"No," Dottie said. Stopping again. This time she waited for Jazzy to get all her questions out.

"Why not?" she asked.

"We've just started."

Sam and Miles nailed two pieces of wood together. Dottie wanted to be hammering too.

"Can I help you when you aren't just started?"

"Maybe," Dottie said. "But if you keep asking questions, we won't get there."

"Okay," Jazzy said. She picked at some grass, then said, "How long does it take to build a tree house?"

"I don't know. I haven't built one before."

"If I made a tree house, I would be done."

"Don't you have somewhere to be?" Dottie asked.

"No," Jazzy said.

Sam and Miles banged some more wood together. It seemed to Dottie like Jazzy had run out of questions, so Dottie prepared her nail, lifted her hammer, and was about to bring it down when Jazzy said, "When will it be done?"

Dottie took a deep breath. "When we finish it," she said.

"When will that be?"

"When we're done."

"Can I go in it when you're done?"

"Sure, but we'll never finish it if you keep asking questions."

"Why?" Jazzy asked.

"Don't you want to bother Dad?"

"No." Jazzy shook her head.

Dottie stared at Jazzy.

"What?" Jazzy said.

"I'm just waiting," Dottie said.

"For what?" asked Jazzy.

"For you to ask another question," Dottie said.

"I don't have any more," Jazzy said.

Dottie placed the hammer on the nail and lifted the hammer into the air, pausing for a split second.

"Why are you making a floor?" Jazzy asked.

Dottie dropped the hammer, which luckily didn't hit any toes. "Can you help me out here?" Dottie turned to Sam, who was a champion at answering Jazzy's questions.

"We're making a floor because we need something to stand on," Sam said.

"But you have something to stand on."

"Not until we make the floor," Sam said.

"What about the ground? Can't you stand on the ground?" Jazzy jumped up and down.

"We could stand on the ground," Sam said. "But we want a floor."

"Why do you want a floor if you don't have a tree?"

Miles looked up. "How many questions do you have?"

Jazzy shrugged. "Maybe a million?"

Sam nodded. "It runs in their family."

"Burping runs in my family," Miles said.

"Mine too," Sam said, and then he and Miles both burped out the alphabet to prove it.

After the burping, Jazzy forgot all about the floor and went off to learn how to burp, leaving the three of them to work on the platform for the rest of the afternoon.

Miles was just about to head home when Grandpa Walter came outside. "What's all the banging?" he asked. The Chock full o'Nuts can was cradled in the crook of his arm.

Dottie shrugged. "Just banging wood together."

"Well, could you do it a little quieter? It woke up Ima and me."

Dottie nodded and Grandpa Walter went back inside but not before stumbling over a piece of wood. "Whoopsie! You okay, Ima?" he asked as he walked through the front door.

Miles stood there for a minute and said, "So, that's your grandpa?"

Dottie nodded. She waited for him to ask about the can, or about Grandpa Walter talking to the can, but she didn't need to worry because just then Miles's mom called on his phone and told him to come home.

He hopped on his bike and took off. "See you tomorrow . . . unless the zombies get you!" he hollered over his shoulder, and biked fast until he was a safe distance from Zombie House and then yelled really loudly, "Not that I believe in zombies! Because I don't!"

Dottie and Sam looked at each other.

"How can he not believe in zombies?" Dottie asked.

Sam shrugged. "No idea," he said as he turned to go home too.

Dottie stood alone with the platform, realizing that for the first time in ages, she felt happy. She knew she was right about the tree house. It did make her happy.

Now all she had to do was figure out how to make Grandpa Walter happy and everything would be perfect.

27. Too Scary?

The next morning, Sam and Dottie were almost at school when Miles caught up to them. They had been cracking themselves up with a Truth or Fake about leeches sucking out all of a person's blood. Dottie doubled over laughing as Sam described how, once the leech was done with the blood, it moved on to the bones. "Until all that was left of the person was their skin," he said. "And they looked like a bedsheet waving in the wind."

Dottie loved this Truth or Fake so much. It was gross and funny at the same time.

This meant she was totally surprised by Miles's head popping between them. "Hey weirdos!"

"Hey weirdo," Dottie said back.

"Are we meeting again today?" Miles asked.

Sam and Dottie nodded.

"Good," Miles said, and ran away like he always did, except this time, he shouted over his shoulder, "See you at school!"

Dottie and Sam watched as he disappeared down the block. "It's incredible how much life can change," Dottie commented. "It's like he's a different person."

"And how fast it changes," Sam added. "It's only been one day."

Even in school, Miles was different. He joined Dottie and Sam in the math games, complimented Sam's bug report, and begged Ms. Agna to keep reading from the read-aloud book about a kid who wants to break a world record.

Then came recess, which consisted of swings and a game of tag. Again, Miles stuck close to Dottie and Sam.

Lunch was typical. Mr. Shark circled the cafeteria, eyeing everyone suspiciously, but Miles made it funnier because every time Mr. Shark passed by, he started humming the theme music to the scary movie *Jaws*.

"Have you watched that?" Dottie asked.

Miles shook his head. "No way. Too scary."

"Too scary?" Dottie was surprised. She still didn't think of Miles as the kind of kid to be scared of anything. It made her think of the time Ima hid a harmonica in the meatloaf. When Grandpa Walter bit into it, Ima shouted, "Surprise!"

"What's this doing here?" Grandpa Walter had asked.

And Ima replied, "Surprises pop up in the most unusual places. That's what makes them a surprise."

That's just how Dottie felt about Miles right now. A total surprise hidden in the meatloaf.

28. Out of Sight, Out of Mind?

Truth or fake?" Dottie asked Sam Batty as the two of them walked out of school. "Miles Huckatony has been taken over by an alien."

"Interesting theory," Sam said.

"Right?" Dottie said. "It's like he's—he's—" She tried to find the word.

"Human?" Sam Batty offered.

"Exactly!"

"And so, the only explanation is that he's been taken over by aliens," Sam said.

It was the most logical explanation Dottie could come up with.

Sam shuffled along beside Dottie. "I don't know if he was taken over by aliens, but I do know I'll take this Miles over the old one."

Dottie couldn't agree more, which was a good thing because

just then Miles Huckatony ran up, barreling into Dottie and Sam like they were bowling pins. "Okay, look," he said. "I've tried not to bring it up all day long, but I can't stand it anymore."

"Can't stand what?" Dottie asked.

"What's in the can your grandpa carries around? And why does he talk to it? He talks to it, right? It sure seems like he talks to it."

Dottie and Sam exchanged looks.

"I get it," Miles continued. "It's a secret, right? I promise not to tell anyone. I waited all day to ask. I didn't even bring it up in school. That's how good I am at keeping secrets."

It wasn't a secret, exactly; it was just hard to talk about.

"Please," Miles begged. "I couldn't think of anything else last night and today. You've got to tell me."

"You might as well," Sam said. "He'll probably find out from Jazzy."

That was true. Dottie swallowed down the alligator rising up in her throat. "It has ashes in it."

"Ashes?" Miles said.

"Of my grandma Ima."

Miles nodded. "That's unusual." He paused and then asked, "Can I see them?"

"See what?" Dottie said.

"The ashes."

"No!" Dottie pulled a face. How could he ask that?

"Come on!" Miles Huckatony pleaded. "I've never seen any ashes before."

"No way."

"Have you seen them?" Miles asked Sam.

Sam shook his head emphatically.

"You've seen them, though," Miles said to Dottie.

"No. I don't want to see the ashes of my grandma. I loved her."

Miles shrugged, then said, "But your grandpa really talks to your dead grandma?"

Dottie suddenly felt a strange sense of protection for Grandpa Walter and the can. "Is there a problem with that?" she asked.

"No, I don't have a problem with it. But I could see some people having a problem. Like your parents. Parents have a problem with everything."

Dottie disagreed. "My parents just want him to be happy."

"That makes sense," Miles blurted out. "I just want my parents to be happy too." He looked at Dottie and Sam and then said, "They fight all the time."

Sam and Dottie got quiet.

"They're getting a divorce," Miles explained.

"Oh," Sam said. "Why?"

"They don't want to fight."

"Will that help?" Dottie asked. She knew kids whose parents weren't together, but she'd never met anyone whose parents were going through it.

Miles said, "It's like when I wasn't allowed on my PlayStation for three days because I read my sister's diary, which between you and me was not that interesting. Anyway, the first day was awful because my PlayStation was sitting out. I kept complaining about not being allowed to play it, so my parents moved it to the basement where I couldn't see it."

Miles Huckatony smiled like that was the end of the story.

Sam Batty looked confused. Dottie felt the same.

"And?" Sam Batty asked.

"And," Miles said. "I stopped thinking about the PlayStation since it wasn't in front of me and started to do a puzzle."

Dottie nodded. "It's like your parents are the PlayStation and they need to be put in the basement."

"Exactly."

"Both of them?" asked Sam, who clearly still didn't get the point. "At the same time?"

"No," Miles said. "One of them goes into the basement and one of them stays upstairs."

"One of them is the PlayStation and one of them is the puzzle?" Sam asked.

Miles explained it one more time.

"Oh," Sam said at last. "Sure. I get it now. Out of sight, out of mind. That's what my parents call it. They did that with me once when I wouldn't stop playing my recorder. The sound got on their nerves. At first, I missed it tons, then I got a keyboard and didn't miss it at all."

Out of sight, out of mind? Dottie turned this over. Could that work for her? Ima was out of sight, but she was definitely not out of mind. And did Dottie really want her out of her mind? Absolutely not! What she wanted was Ima. Here. With her.

No, out of sight, out of mind wasn't for her. Maybe it only worked on certain kinds of problems.

"Yoo-hoo," Sam called after Dottie.

"Earth to Dottie," Miles added with a holler.

Dottie looked around. Sam and Miles were standing way behind her. She was thinking so hard, she had walked right past her house.

"That's funny." Miles giggled. "It's like you've been taken over by aliens and don't remember where you live." Miles giggled some more.

Dottie joined in. It was funny forgetting where she lived. It was also funny being an alien. She hadn't thought she had anything in common with Miles, but maybe they were more similar than she realized.

29. What Do You Need a Railing For?

Dottie and Sam and Miles agreed to meet back at Dottie's house in a half an hour.

As Dottie walked inside, Jazzy shouted at the top of her lungs, "Dottie's home!"

"You don't need to shout," Grandpa Walter said. "Ima and I can hear just fine."

Usually, Dottie's dad met her with a snack, but he wasn't here. Today it was Grandpa Walter and Jazzy and no snack.

"Now that Dottie is home," Grandpa Walter said, "I'm going to have a little rest."

"Bye-bye Ima!" Jazzy waved to the can.

"Where's Dad?" Dottie asked.

"Out," Jazzy said. "Grandpa Walter and I had a coffee date."

"You drank coffee?"

"Yuck, no!" Jazzy made a face. "Warm milk."

Jazzy stood up and did a little tap dance. "You're never going to guess who I have been talking to." Jazzy didn't wait for an answer. "Ima!"

Dottie froze. Jazzy went on. "She sends her love and says she misses me. She misses you too. Also, she wishes she could have a cup of coffee. She really misses coffee. She says not to worry about her. She also thanks you for sharing your room with Grandpa Walter and says it would be nice if you let him paint it green. She says Grandpa Walter has always liked the color green."

Dottie ignored the comment about painting her room. That would never happen. It took Dottie ages to pick out the exact color of blue that she wanted. She wasn't changing it.

"You talked to Ima?"

"She's got a lot to say and luckily Grandpa Walter hears it all because I can't hear a word."

Dottie felt a lump form in her throat—the alligator and his friends were back.

Dottie wanted to talk to Ima. She had so much to tell her. About Sam and the baby, about the tree house and Miles and about school and what she'd learned about dung beetles. In the middle of listing all the topics she wanted to share, she stopped.

Everything stopped.

Everything except one thought. Why could Grandpa Walter talk to Ima and not Dottie?

There were so many things she wanted to share but

couldn't. Her insides hurt like all the animals were scratching and poking and biting and jumping and squeezing all at the same time. Dottie wanted to run away from it, but it was inside her. There was nowhere to go.

And then Jazzy climbed into Dottie's lap. "Can you finish the tree house now? I want somewhere to tap-dance." Jazzy tweaked Dottie's nose, so she'd pay attention. "TREE HOUSE!" she yelled at the top of her lungs.

By the time Sam and Miles arrived a few minutes later, Jazzy was hanging upside down off a lawn chair and Dottie was staring at the platform.

"What are you doing?" Sam asked.

"Trying to decide what we build next," Dottie said.

"That's easy," Miles said. "A railing."

"What do you need a railing for?" Jazzy asked.

"To keep us safe," Miles said.

"What's it keeping us safe from?" Jazzy asked. Her eyeballs bulged from hanging upside down.

"From falling out," Miles said.

"But your tree house is on the ground."

"Eventually it will be in a tree," Dottie said.

"When?" Jazzy asked.

Dottie had the same question.

"Soon," Sam said optimistically.

Jazzy flipped back upright. "I hope it's soon. A tree house on the ground is boring."

Dottie agreed. But one question stuck in her mind. How

could Grandpa Walter be sad when he was the only one who got to talk to Ima? It was so obvious to Dottie. How could her parents not see it?

"Don't worry about Grandpa Walter," Sam said, knowing exactly what was on Dottie's mind. "Something will happen. Something always happens."

And because Sam was so smart, and had troubles of his own, Dottie listened to him.

The railing they finally built looked like no railing Dottie had ever seen, but when they leaned against it, it didn't fall over. And what else was a railing for?

30. Why Did She Feel So Miserable?

After dinner, Grandpa Walter insisted on helping with the dishes. "If I don't cook, I have to clean." Dottie's mom put him to work scrubbing pots at the sink. No one could break metal pots. Although it was amazing how much water could splash, how many pots could tumble to the floor, and how much soap could get squeezed out. Everywhere.

Dottie, her mom, and her dad took over the cleaning up as Grandpa Walter sat down to play some cards. "Dottie," he said. "I wanted to talk to you."

Dottie was wiping the counter. Maybe he was going to tell her parents that he was happy. That he was ready to leave. For a brief moment, Dottie felt hopeful.

Grandpa Walter carried on. "You know how much Ima loved the color green?"

Dottie nodded. (Green was Ima's favorite color.)

"And you know how much I love green."

Dottie nodded. (She actually only knew this because Jazzy had said so earlier.)

"Well, we were thinking about painting your room."

"We who?" Dottie's dad asked, looking concerned.

"Your mother and me," Grandpa Walter said.

"Mom and you?" Dottie's dad repeated.

The earlier conversation with Jazzy came roaring back to Dottie. Dottie frowned. This conversation had nothing to do with Grandpa Walter being happy and everything to do with painting her room.

"Dad." Dottie's dad sounded worried. "I think we should talk about this privately."

"Why?" Grandpa Walter said. "It's just a coat of paint. You can always change it back."

Grandpa Walter was right. Dottie could always change it back, but that wasn't the problem. The problem was that she couldn't build her tree house in the tree until he left, and he wasn't leaving until he was happy. And she didn't see how painting a room would make him happy. Of course, if it did, the answer was simple. But what if it didn't? Dottie's head was spinning, and she didn't know what to do. How could she decide?

Grandpa Walter said, "Ima thinks it's a great idea."

"Ima," Dottie repeated. And thought, *What would Ima do?* Dottie knew immediately the answer to this question.

"If it will make you happy," Dottie said. "Then yes, you can paint my room."

"Thanks Dottie," Grandpa Walter said. And he smiled his tiny, crooked smile. (Proof to Dottie that he was happier than her parents gave him credit for.)

Dottie walked upstairs, leaving her dad and mom and Grandpa Walter. She stood in her doorway. Looking at her room. She felt so befuddled, which was Sam's much better word for confused.

She wanted Grandpa Walter to be happy. She really did. So how come she felt so rotten?

31. Did Something Happen?

The next morning Dottie walked outside expecting (as always) to see Sam. And sure enough, there he was. But someone else was there too.

Miles Huckatony!

What was he doing there?

Sam seemed to read Dottie's thoughts. "I asked him to walk with us," he said. In lots of ways, Sam and Ima were different, but also in lots of ways they were similar. They both liked word games. They both liked chocolate ice cream. And they were both generous. Generous because they didn't like people to be left out.

Sam was also like Ima because he could tell right away that something was wrong with Dottie. Just like Ima would have known. "What's wrong?" he asked.

"Don't ask." Dottie heaved her backpack onto her shoulders.

"Did something happen?" Sam asked.

"I told you not to ask."

"Is it bad?" Miles asked.

"I don't want to talk about it."

"You know you'll feel better if you talk about it," Sam said.

"Fine," Dottie said, stopping in her tracks. "Grandpa Walter is painting my room."

"Oh!" Miles gasped. "That is bad."

Sam elbowed him.

"Ow," Miles grunted. "Why'd you do that?"

"Because you don't have to say everything you think out loud." Sam turned back to Dottie and asked, "Why is he painting it?"

"Ima likes the color green."

Miles's eyebrows popped up. "You mean, your grandma Ima? The one in the can?"

Dottie nodded.

"What color is your room now?" Miles asked.

"Blue."

Miles nodded. "I like green more too."

Sam elbowed Miles again. (A little harder this time.)

"Ow." Miles rubbed his arm. "Did I do it again?"

Sam nodded. "But maybe he'll paint the room and get happy and leave. Right?"

"You think?" Miles asked. "Seems like someone paints a room and that means they're staying."

Dottie sighed and started walking again.

Sam frowned at Miles. "You know, sometimes you not only say everything out loud, but you are also the voice of doom."

Miles shrugged. "You call it doom; I call it honesty."

At school, paying attention was impossible. Dottie's mind drifted back to Grandpa Walter. Would he be happy now? He had to be. But what if Miles was right? What if Grandpa Walter never left and Dottie never built the tree house in the tree and for the rest of her life she had an alligator, a porcupine, an octopus, and a kangaroo living inside her?

No. Dottie wouldn't let that happen.

Ima believed that every problem had a solution and Ima was never wrong. Dottie would have her tree house.

32. He's Doing What?

As soon as Dottie walked back into her house at the end of the day, her dad raced over to her. "Dottie, I—"

Before he could finish, Grandpa Walter appeared. He was whistling. Dottie never heard him whistle before. "I didn't know you could whistle," she said.

Grandpa Walter shrugged. "There's lots you don't know about me."

That was true. She had known him her whole life and she still didn't feel like she knew him at all. She didn't even know for sure if he was happy or sad.

"Dot," her dad said. "I'm sorry."

"About what?" Dottie asked.

"About—"

Right then, Jazzy and her mom paraded in bearing a bucket of paint, brushes, and rollers. Immediately, Dottie understood what her dad was sorry about.

"I wanted to carry it," Grandpa Walter announced. "But Miriam was worried I might drop something. I'm not *that* clumsy."

Dottie's mom gave her dad a look as if to say, *Oh yes, he is.*

"Let's bring everything upstairs," Grandpa Walter said.

"Grandpa Walter?" Jazzy ran over. "Can I carry Ima?"

"No, no, no. It's best if I do that. We don't want to drop her."

"I wouldn't drop her." Jazzy frowned.

"Jazzy, you are not carrying the can," Dottie's dad said.

Jazzy let out a deep sigh. "Then can I help paint?" Jazzy looked at Dottie. "He's starting today."

Dottie didn't think it would be so soon.

Grandpa Walter turned to Dottie. "It's you, Dottie, who I have to thank."

"Me?"

"Absolutely," he said. "It was watching you and your friends build that contraption out front that gave me the idea."

"It did?" Dottie asked.

"Listening to all that banging reminded me that I can do things too." And then he smiled. No, thought Dottie, not smiled, *beamed*. That's how Sam would describe it. Beaming was better than smiling, so that must mean he was happy. So happy that her parents would ask him to leave, and Dottie, Sam, and Miles could start building the tree house where it belonged (in a tree). And maybe Dottie would keep her room green. Who knew? After all, Ima liked the color. Dottie imagined it all and she had to admit that it made her beam too. It was all going to work out.

"Hey, Grandpa Walter," Jazzy said, reaching up and tugging his sleeve. "After you paint, you won't go anywhere, will you?"

Grandpa Walter looked surprised by this question.

Dottie looked surprised by the question. Even Dottie's dad and mom looked surprised by the question.

"Jazzy," Grandpa Walter said, kneeling down close to her. "When that room is painted, I'll never want to leave."

"What?" Dottie asked. "Never leave?" A stampede was taking place in Dottie's heart. She never thought an octopus could be part of a stampede (but it was true). She also never thought building a tree house would be so hard! (But that was true too.)

Dottie's dad leaned over and whispered, "Don't worry. He doesn't mean it."

How could he not mean it? He just said it.

Grandpa Walter stood up. "Now, I'm going to go outside for the big ladder."

A look of terror flashed across Dottie's dad's face, and he dashed out to help him.

That, at least, Dottie understood. Grandpa Walter and a ladder seemed like a very bad idea. Definitely worse than painting Dottie's room.

33. What's Brainstorming?

There was no escape from the sounds of Grandpa Walter painting. Dottie listened from the kitchen to the crashes, to the grunts, to the ooopses, and interspersed between all that was Grandpa Walter whistling a cheerful, zippy little tune.

Compelled was the word Sam used when he watched five zombie movies in one weekend. He didn't mean to watch that many, but he couldn't stop himself.

Dottie felt compelled to solve the problem of the tree house. But how? She paced back and forth, hoping that something would come to her. Nothing.

From upstairs Grandpa Walter exclaimed, "Oh, Ima! This was a good idea."

Ima. Dottie gulped. If Ima were here, she would know what to do. And right then, Dottie thought of the time Ima was trying to decide which cake to have for her birthday. "Can I only have one?" she joked, and then started to make a list.

"It's a brainstorm list," she explained. "The more ideas you have, the easier it is to decide what you want."

Dottie slapped her forehead. That was it!

Dottie was so compelled by the idea of brainstorming that even though Sam and Miles weren't supposed to be there for another half hour, she called them and made them come as soon as possible.

When they both arrived, Dottie told them about Grandpa Walter painting and whistling and beaming.

"Nice word," Sam said.

"I thought you'd appreciate it," Dottie said.

"So, he's happy?" Sam asked.

"Oh yeah, he's happy," Dottie said.

"Isn't that what you wanted?" Miles asked.

"Yup, but he isn't leaving."

"What?" Sam said.

"He told Jazzy he wants to stay!"

Miles frowned. "It's hard when you lose your room." He looked like he really meant it.

"This isn't about losing my room," Dottie said, a little frustrated. "This is about building a tree house."

"But, to build the tree house, you need the tree, which means you need your room," Sam said.

"Yes," Dottie agreed reluctantly. "Which is why we need a new plan."

"How do we do that?" Miles asked.

"We brainstorm," Dottie said.

"Oh," Sam perked up. "I like brainstorming."

"What's brainstorming?" Miles asked.

"How do you think anything in this world gets done?" Sam asked Miles.

"People fight and whoever is the loudest wins." Miles shrugged.

Dottie had to admit Miles had a point. Some people did do that.

"But that's not a great way to decide anything," Sam said. "In brainstorming we think of as many solutions as possible and choose the best one."

"I don't know if it'll work, but it sounds more fun than yelling. Where do we start?"

"We decide on a goal," Dottie explained.

"That's easy," Sam said. "We want to build a tree house."

"Is that the goal?" Miles asked. "Or is it you want your room back?"

Dottie was as confused as they were. "I need my room for the tree house," she said, thinking through the problem. "In order to have my room, Grandpa Walter needs to leave. And my mom and dad think he won't leave until he's happy. So, the goal has to be to make him happy."

"Are you sure you shouldn't make him miserable?" Miles suggested.

Dottie shook her head. Even though his visit was delaying her tree house and he was painting her perfectly blue room green, she could never do that to Grandpa Walter.

"Okay," Sam said. "So we need to come up with an idea to make Grandpa Walter happy."

"Oh, I have one!" Miles said. "Give him candy! Candy makes everyone happy."

Dottie shook her head. "I don't think he likes candy."

"Remember," Sam said. "The first rule of brainstorming is every idea is a good idea."

"How do you know that?" Dottie asked.

"I remember Ima explaining it."

"You knew Ima?" Miles asked.

"Sure I knew Ima," Sam said. "I've lived next door to Dottie half my life."

"I wish I had known Ima."

Dottie got very quiet. The alligator flipped in her stomach and the rest of the menagerie joined it. She wished Miles had known Ima too.

"Oh!" Miles shouted. "I've got another one. Give him a PlayStation."

"Dye his hair green," Sam said.

"Play tag," Dottie said.

"Play freeze tag," Miles said.

"Play monster tag," Sam said.

"Play zombie tag!" Dottie shouted.

"No zombies," Miles said.

"Send him a treasure map!" Sam suggested.

"Throw a dance party!" Miles said.

"A dance party?" Dottie and Sam said at the same time.

"What about it?" Miles asked. "Dancing makes me happy."

Dancing made Dottie and Sam happy too. Miles sure was a surprise.

After another five minutes of brainstorming, Dottie dropped to the ground. As fun as this was, they were getting nowhere. "Why is this so hard?"

"Because nothing will make Grandpa Walter happy?" Miles said, sitting down beside her.

"I just want to build the tree house!" Dottie wailed.

"And we will," Sam said, plunking down next to Dottie and Miles.

"How?" Dottie pleaded. "How?"

Sam frowned, deep in concentration, and then said, "What would Ima do?"

Dottie didn't have to think about this. She knew exactly what Ima would do. "Ima never tiptoed around Grandpa Walter. She didn't care if it bothered him. She'd just do it. Like when she took up the violin." Dottie giggled. "She gave Grandpa Walter a pair of earmuffs and told him to get used to it." Dottie paused, thinking about this memory. "Learning violin is very screechy."

"My mom and Ima would have liked each other," Miles said. "You know how my mom is going through a hard time? Because of my dad and her?"

Dottie and Sam nodded.

"She says it's very annoying because everyone keeps acting like she's super delicate and fragile. She hates that and wants to be treated like her regular old self."

Sam sat up straighter. "Oh!" he gasped. "That's it."

"What's it?" Dottie asked.

Sam continued, "Right now, everyone is acting like Grandpa Walter is a guest who needs special care, right?"

Dottie nodded.

"But he shouldn't be treated like that. You need to treat him like Ima would or like Miles's mom wants to be—like a regular person."

Dottie pulled at some grass and thought. "So, instead of trying to make him happy by being nice, we make him happy by treating him like ordinary Grandpa Walter?"

Sam nodded enthusiastically.

Dottie kept talking. "And we build the tree house whether he is happy or sad and whether he stays or goes?"

"Exactly," Sam said.

"Wow," Dottie said. "I never thought of it that way. But I guess it is what Ima would do. And if she would do it, then so can we."

It was too late to get started, so they agreed to start the next day. Right after school.

As Sam and Miles left, Sam turned back to Dottie. "This was the best brainstorming session ever."

"There's no stopping us!" Miles said as he ran home.

And thanks to the fact that there wasn't a single animal fussing, fighting, crushing, or even jumping inside her, Dottie truly agreed.

34. What Tree House?

Dottie knew she'd have to tell her parents that she was moving ahead with her plan—*mission*—to build the tree house. But when she came back into the house, they were too busy cleaning up a paint spill to talk. After dinner, they were also busy— this time with driving to buy more paint for Grandpa Walter because of the spill.

By the time her parents were back, Dottie was too sleepy to talk. In the middle of the night, Dottie woke up to Jazzy tossing and turning so much that she decided sleeping on the floor was a better choice. When she woke up, she didn't care that MacFurry's claws were tangled in her hair. (That was a first.) And then, by the time she untangled her hair (which took longer than she thought), it was time to leave for school. So, it would have to wait until this afternoon.

It was a long slow day at school and not even dung beetles made it go faster. Dottie, Sam, and Miles counted along to the ticking clock, until they were free. Dottie still needed to tell her father that they were building the tree house today, so Sam suggested Miles stay at his house until Dottie was done.

Dottie found her dad in the kitchen with Jazzy, who was licking gooey stuff off her fingers.

Dottie cleared her throat. "Dad, I'm building the tree house and there's nothing you can do about it."

"YES!" Jazzy said, leaping from her chair. "Finally!"

"Hmm," he said. "Didn't we decide to wait?"

"I've waited long enough."

That's when Jazzy started to tap-dance. "There's a floor, and there's a railing, and I will tap-dance out there so Grandpa Walter can nap. And I will not bother Dottie because I want her to finish. It's going to be fantastic!"

Jazzy tapped around her father.

"Please—" Dottie struggled to say more because, at that very moment, those four animals crowded into her neck, blocking any other sound from escaping.

Dottie's dad sighed deeply. "I don't understand why this tree house is so important, but I see that it is. So yes, you can build it."

"I can?" Dottie jumped into her dad's arms.

"If Grandpa Walter complains, I'll send him to you."

If Dottie's dad knew about the alligator, porcupine, octopus, and kangaroo, he would also know that Grandpa Walter's complaints were the least of her worries.

35. What Do We Do Now?

Dottie, Sam, and Miles dragged the platform around the house to the tree—accidentally pulling off the railing along the way.

Sam looked at it and then said, "Better to find out it wasn't sturdy now than up in the tree."

Dottie had to agree, but she still wished it hadn't broken.

It was at the bottom of the tree that they found they had another problem.

"It doesn't wrap around the tree," Sam said.

"How could we forget a hole for the trunk?" Dottie asked.

"What do we do now?" Miles asked.

This tree house would not be stopped because of a little mistake like that. Dottie was determined. "We build another platform," she said. "Put them both in the tree and connect them."

And that's what they did. For the rest of the afternoon, they focused all their energy on building another platform. When it came time to get it into the tree, all three of them realized that as much as they didn't want it, they needed help.

Dottie's dad obliged, which they all agreed was a good thing because he actually knew about nuts and bolts and safety. He also found another ladder and leaned it up against the tree so they could get in and out.

Dottie had imagined how much fun it would be to build a tree house, but this was so much better than she dreamed. There was something about climbing up and down the ladder, carrying the wood, pounding, hammering, and drilling that filled her up with joy. Even pretending to whack her finger with the hammer had her doubled over in giggles.

And best of all, there wasn't a writhing alligator, a poking porcupine, a squeezing octopus, or a shuddering kangaroo in sight. They were gone! Gone! Gone! And Dottie was sure that now they would never come back.

36. What's All the Racket?

Dottie, Sam, and Miles were almost finished with the platform when the window from Dottie's bedroom opened, and Grandpa Walter leaned out. It was clear from the amount of paint covering him that there had been a few more accidents. "What's all the racket? We can't nap with all this noise."

Dottie froze. Even though she knew that this is what Ima would do, she was still scared to go through with it.

Sam whispered, "Pretend you're Ima."

"I'm Ima," Dottie repeated.

Miles whispered, "Treat him like you would anyone else."

She took a deep breath and said, "We're building a tree house."

"A tree house?" Grandpa Walter said, sounding surprised. "Weren't you building that out front?"

"Yes," Dottie answered. "We were."

Grandpa Walter nodded. "A tree house in a tree makes a

lot more sense." He held up the Chock full o'Nuts can and said, "Look, Ima! They're building a tree house." And then returned inside.

"Well," Miles said after a few moments. "That went better than I expected."

"What did you expect?" Dottie asked.

Miles shrugged. "You never know what to expect when you're dealing with grown-ups."

Sam nodded. "So true, Miles, so true." Sam had a faraway look that told Dottie he was thinking about his own parents. He certainly never expected to be a big brother.

Dottie hadn't expected Ima to die. She hadn't expected to build a tree house. And she sure hadn't expected Grandpa Walter to move in. Was there anything in life that *could* be expected?

All of a sudden, there was a *CRASH, SMASH, BANG, BOING* from Dottie's room and then Grandpa Walter hollered, "I'm okay. Nothing's hurt."

Dottie looked at Sam and Miles. "Maybe there are *some* things that can be expected. Or, at least, one thing if we're talking about Grandpa Walter."

Sam and Miles laughed and then they returned to working on the tree house.

37. Lovable?

By the time Sam and Miles were called back to their homes, the platform was complete, and they were ready to start another railing (definitely stronger than the last one). Later that night, as Dottie walked out of the bathroom on her way to bed, Grandpa Walter called out. "Dottie?" The door to Dottie's old room was closed, and Dottie wondered how he knew it was her. Yet another Grandpa Walter mystery. "I need your help!"

It sounded urgent, so Dottie raced over and flung open the door. This was the first time Dottie had encountered the new color of her room. It made her blink. It wasn't terrible, but it wasn't blue.

"Dottie, come here." Grandpa Walter motioned from the bed, where he was sitting next to a strange lump that was curled up around the Chock full o'Nuts can. A loud humming sound emanated from the lump as Grandpa Walter petted it.

Emanated was the word Sam used when he described the smell after being skunked once. It was a beautiful word for something incredibly stinky. Maybe that's why Dottie thought of it now. Because it was suddenly clear that the humming emanating from the lump wasn't any old humming. It was actually purring, which meant that the lump wasn't any old lump either. It was MacFurry.

This was stinkier than a skunk stinking. After all the attention Dottie had given that cat, what was he doing cuddling up with Grandpa Walter?

"Traitor," Dottie growled under her breath.

"Dottie," Grandpa Walter said. "My glasses slipped down on the floor. I didn't want to disturb the cat. Could you grab them?" He pointed to the floor.

"You didn't want to disturb MacFurry?" Dottie asked, picking up the glasses and handing them to Grandpa Walter. MacFurry was usually the one doing the disturbing.

"He's such a sweetie."

"A sweetie?" Were they talking about the same cat?

"How did I never realize how lovable he is?"

"Lovable?" Had MacFurry changed overnight?

Grandpa Walter picked up the book that lay beside him and started to read out loud again.

A tightness in her chest confused Dottie. Building the tree house was supposed to stop that. So why was she feeling it now? It didn't make any sense. But neither did Grandpa Walter describing MacFurry as lovable, and he had done just that.

No, no. Dottie shook her head. She was just tired after a long and happy day of building. All she needed was to sleep. That's what Ima would have told her. "Everything looks better after a good night's sleep," Ima always said. And Ima was never wrong. (Never.)

38. Could This Day Get Any Better?

The next morning Dottie woke up rested and ready for a fantastic Friday. It was fantastic because after school there would be nothing stopping her from building the tree house.

As they walked to school, Sam, Miles, and Dottie planned out the whole weekend.

"So, I suggest after school today," Dottie said, "we work on the tree house."

"Good idea," said Sam.

"And then on Saturday," Miles added, "we could work on the tree house."

"Brilliant." Dottie nodded in approval.

"I don't know about you two," Sam added, "but on Sunday I'll be busy working on the tree house."

It was not a complicated plan, but it made Dottie happy. So happy that she didn't even mind being in school or having Mr. Shark advise her to "Talk less and eat more."

When the end of the day rolled around, they ran straight to Dottie's house. Miles called his mom and told her he was with Dottie and Sam. Sam told his mom he was with Dottie and Miles. And Dottie told her dad that they would be building the tree house.

Dottie was amazed by how happy she felt. Happy pounding and hammering and sawing and giggling. So happy that she truly forgot about Grandpa Walter. At least until he stuck his head out her window and said, "How long are you going to be pounding away like that? We're trying to nap."

Dottie was so happy that she just smiled and said, "Oh sorry. We'll try to be quieter."

"Quieter?" Grandpa Walter grumped. "I meant stop."

But they didn't stop, and they wouldn't stop. Not until the railing was completely finished and wrapped the whole way around the platform.

Once that was done, they invited Jazzy, who had been patiently waiting below, to climb up. As soon as her feet hit the platform she started to tap, and she tapped, tapped, tapped all over the tree house singing at the tops of her lungs. "I LOVE LOVE LOVE LOVE THE TREE TREE TREE TREE HOUSE!"

After Jazzy left to help with dinner, Dottie, Sam, and Miles stayed, dangling their legs through the slats of the railings.

"Could this day get any better?" Miles asked.

"I don't think so," Sam said.

"It's the best day I've had in months," Miles said.

Dottie agreed completely. She really did. And yet—she didn't feel the way she wanted to. The way she thought she would. Why was that?

Before she could think of an answer, her dad came out and said that it was time for Sam and Miles to go home.

As they climbed down the ladder, Dottie heard Grandpa Walter's whistling drifting out the window. He was whistling a song Ima used to sing all about imagining peace and suddenly she was overtaken by a gnawing in her belly, by a tightness in her throat, and by a definite creeping like tentacles stretching out inside her. Dottie paused. And was that a bison that just joined the group? Unbelievable!

Miles's mom was waiting in her car. "See you tomorrow." He waved and took off.

But Sam stopped. "Are you okay?" he asked.

Dottie was determined to be okay. She had to be okay. The tree house was making her okay. She forced a smile and said, "Yeah. Totally okay. This day couldn't get any better."

Sam smiled back and ran home, leaving Dottie worried that if a day couldn't get any better, did that mean it could only get worse?

Dottie shivered. The idea was unbearable.

39. A Load of What?

On Saturday morning, Dottie woke up in a bad mood. She couldn't blame Jazzy because she had stayed in her own bunk all night. And she couldn't blame MacFurry because, thanks to Grandpa Walter, he no longer bit her. That left one option: Why was that pesky alligator still snapping around? Why wouldn't the rest of the animals leave Dottie alone? Working on the tree house yesterday had been so fun! So what the heck was she doing wrong? It made Dottie grouchy, grumpy, and grumbly.

Dottie climbed into the tree house to wait for Sam and Miles. By the time they arrived, she felt as prickly as the porcupine that was poking her insides. "Where have you been?" she asked impatiently as they climbed up.

"I was looking for this." Miles beamed and held up the rope ladder he brought from home. (Rope ladders were way better than regular ones.)

Sam shrugged. "My mom needed help putting the crib together."

"Yoo-hoo!" Dottie's mom called from below. "I'll be here in case you need me." She pulled up a lawn chair and settled into it while she graded papers.

Now that they had a platform and the railing, they needed to start on the room. Dottie, Sam, and Miles lugged more wood up to the platform, but after that they weren't sure what to do. Luckily, Dottie's mom was a genius at many things (including carpentry). She showed them how to place and nail the pieces together so the structure wouldn't fall down on top of them.

Dottie found as she worked that her mood lightened, and she almost forgot that there was a bothersome pack of animals living inside her. But then out of nowhere, they would come back in full force. That was why she sometimes hammered like she was happy and sometimes hammered like she wasn't.

During one particularly stressful moment, Sam squinted up at Dottie and said, "Truth or fake? A lizard's brain explodes when it gets overheated in the sun."

Dottie knew what Sam was trying to do by changing the subject for her, so she pulled herself together and said, "It must be true."

"Fake," Miles said, waving them away with a hand. "All the stuff you say is fake."

This tipped Dottie over the edge. Why did Miles have to be such a grump about Truth or Fake? "You think everything is a load of hooey," Dottie huffed.

"A load of hooey." Sam laughed. "That's funny."

"What does that even mean?" Miles asked.

"*Hooey*," Dottie explained, "means a load of nonsense. Ima used to say it. You never knew what might be a load of hooey to Ima. Usually it was anything she didn't like."

"You know what I think is hooey?" Miles asked.

"What?"

"The zombies across the street."

Dottie was horrified.

"The way I see it is," Miles said, "if there were zombies in that house, they would have come out by now and eaten us because there's nothing to eat in there."

Dottie froze. She had never thought about it like that.

"Miles," Sam said. "You can't say things like that."

"Why not?" he asked.

"Because," Dottie sputtered. "If you don't believe in zombies, what do you believe?"

"Why do I have to believe in zombies?" Miles asked.

"Isn't it obvious?" Sam asked, laughing. "Because believing in zombies is way more fun than not."

Miles let out an exasperated sigh. "Sometimes you two drive me bananas!"

"Sometimes," Dottie snapped, "you drive me bananas too."

Before Miles could respond, the skies opened up and it started to rain. Not a soft, sweet, gentle rain, but a powerhouse kind of rain that was like standing in a shower.

And for some unknown reason, Dottie burst into giggles. She couldn't stop. She just stood there laughing and laughing. She couldn't even speak; she was laughing so hard. And the rain pelted down in buckets, but Dottie laughed through it all. Sam and Miles looked from Dottie to each other, and then they too began to giggle. And once they started, their giggles turned into guffaws and hee-haws until all three toppled over, doubled up in hysterics as the rain poured down, drenching them to their very bones.

40. Why Can't You Talk?

Dottie, Sam, and Miles sat in the kitchen drinking hot chocolate and snuggled in towels and drying out after their mad dash in from the rain.

"You know," Miles said, returning to their earlier conversation. "I do believe in things. Like, I believe that you are building this tree house for some big reason that you haven't told me about."

Dottie blinked and put down her mug. She hadn't expected him to say that. How did he even know that? Sam would never have told him.

She dropped her head down onto the table, painfully aware that the whole point of building the tree house was to fix her feelings, and it wasn't working. It wasn't working at all.

"Dottie," Sam said. "Do you want to tell him what's going on?"

Dottie shook her head.

"I think it will help," Sam said.

"Whatever it is," Miles said, "I promise not to say anything wrong."

It wasn't that Dottie didn't want to talk. She couldn't. If Sam and Miles knew there was an octopus nestled in her mouth, they would have understood why she stayed silent.

"Can I tell him?" Sam asked. Dottie nodded back.

Sam explained to Miles all about what happened after Ima died. How sad Dottie was and how she tried everything to shake the sadness away, but nothing worked. How, at last, she decided to build a tree house. Because that's what Ima would have done.

As Sam told the story, the animals inside her turned Dottie's stomach into a trampoline. It did not feel good.

"Now I get it," Miles said. "But why can't you talk?"

Dottie took a deep breath. "Do you know what it's like to have an alligator, porcupine, octopus, and kangaroo living inside you?"

"Yes," Miles said. "Yes, I do."

Sam nodded. "Me too."

Dottie hadn't considered that they both knew that feeling and now that she knew, she wished, with all her heart, that none of them did.

41. Is It the Can?

"Okay," Miles said, standing up and pacing back and forth. "Let me get this straight. The problem is you are sad. And you thought the tree house would fix it." He paused and stared at her.

Dottie nodded.

"I'm not sure I see the logic, but you are Dottie Bing, and you have a different way of thinking from most of us."

Dottie squinted her eyes at Miles.

"That wasn't an insult," Miles said. "It's something I like about you." He began to march across the room once more.

Sam jumped up and joined Miles in the walking. "Does this help you think?" Sam asked.

Miles shrugged. "My dad does this when he's thinking hard, so it can't hurt. But back to the problem, how do we fix Dottie from being sad?"

Miles paced back and forth. Sam paced back and forth. Dottie felt left out, so she stood up and joined them.

Miles jerked to a sudden stop. "I've got an idea. When my parents took away my PlayStation, I was sad. Really sad. But after a while, I stopped missing it."

"We've talked about the PlayStation before," Dottie said. "It didn't help."

"Maybe we were thinking about it wrong," Sam said.

"How else could we think about it?" Dottie asked.

"Is there something besides Ima that makes you sad?" Sam wondered.

Dottie shook her head. "Only Ima."

"Can you list the times you were sad?" Miles urged.

Dottie sighed and then counted off the most recent times she felt sad. "When Grandpa Walter arrived with the can. When Grandpa Walter made extra cups of coffee for the can and read to it and played cards with it and then when the can told him to paint my room—that made me sad and mad and it's all Ima."

"This might sound weird," Sam said, slowly. "But what if it's the Chock full o'Nuts can that makes you sad?"

"Ohhh," Miles gasped as his eyes got big and he stood up taller. "That's your PlayStation."

"The can?" Dottie asked.

"It has to be," Sam said.

Dottie wasn't sure but then again, Sam was never wrong—and also, it was true, every time she was sad, it was with the can.

"So, if the can is my PlayStation that means—" She cut herself off.

"You have to take the can." Sam finished Dottie's sentence.

"The can," Miles repeated. "Why didn't we think of that sooner?"

"I can't take the can," Dottie said.

"You have to take the can," Miles said. "There's no other way. You have to do what my parents did. Hide the can and don't look at it."

"But I can't take the can. It's full of ashes."

Miles shook his head. "Pretend it's a PlayStation."

"He's right," Sam said. "You'll do just like Miles's parents did—as soon as you're happy, you'll give it back to him." He paused and then continued, "Of course, the biggest difference is that you have to take the can without anyone knowing about it."

"That's stealing!" Dottie gasped.

"Not stealing," Miles said. "Borrowing."

Dottie peered straight into Miles's face. "Miles," she said. "Do you promise that you really changed after the PlayStation was taken away?"

"Oh yeah, I totally changed. My parents were right. Out of sight. Out of mind. Really, I'm glad my parents took it away. Now I don't obsess over it. I can play and stop when I want. And on top of that, if they hadn't hidden it away, we never would have hung out. You two are way better than the Play-

Station." A second later, Miles frowned. "I would hate it if we couldn't hang out anymore."

Sam smiled. "That will never happen."

"You know," Dottie said, interrupting Sam and Miles, "now that I think about it, I am actually helping Grandpa Walter too."

"How are you doing that?" Miles asked.

"If the can makes me sad, then it must make him sad too. Once the can is out of sight and out of mind, we will both be happy and then he will go home, and when he goes home, I can return the can. This is a very good plan. And it's all thanks to you two."

Sam said, "We are pretty great, aren't we?"

Miles blushed, which showed Dottie that their friendship meant as much to him as it did to her. In a million years, Dottie never thought she would say something like that. But she also never thought she'd be taking the Chock full o'Nuts can from Grandpa Walter.

42. Where Was It?

Taking the can was not as easy as Dottie hoped because Grandpa Walter never let it out of his sight. Five days passed since they had decided on the mission and a lot had happened. MacFurry had moved in with Grandpa Walter. Dottie, Sam, and Miles had stopped building the tree house because Dottie couldn't have too many plans (missions) at one time. And last but not least, over the past five days, Dottie had arrived at the incredible idea of building a bridge between her room and the tree house (once they started to work on it again).

Unfortunately, over the past five days Dottie had failed to take the can. But she refused to give up. This mission was far too important.

Then on Friday morning, Dottie's luck changed. She was on her way downstairs when Grandpa Walter came out of his room with MacFurry close on his heels.

"MacFurry," he said. "You have to be careful. I'm a real klutz."

MacFurry twisted between Grandpa Walter's legs, following Grandpa Walter into the bathroom.

Dottie watched the door close. Grandpa Walter walked into the bathroom with MacFurry but without the Chock full o'Nuts can? Where was it?

Dottie tiptoed to her room (Grandpa Walter's). The Chock full o'Nuts can was right there. On the nightstand. Next to the bed.

She reached out and, for the first time ever, held the Chock full o'Nuts can.

For a moment she stood there. Waiting for something. What? For Ima to speak to her? For an electric shock to shoot out so she dropped it? Nothing happened.

And then she heard the rattle of the bathroom door. Grandpa Walter! She dashed away with the can, amazed that she finally could thank MacFurry for something besides scratching her.

43. How Long?

Dottie stuffed the Chock full o'Nuts can into her backpack, and, clutching her backpack tightly, flew out of her room, down the stairs, hollered a loud goodbye, and ran out the door.

She waited for Grandpa Walter to yell.

She waited for her mom to yell that Grandpa Walter was yelling.

In a weird way, she even waited for Ima to yell.

None of that happened.

Once outside, the only noise was the pounding of Dottie's feet on the pavement as she ran to Sam's house. While waiting for Sam, she smooshed the Chock full o'Nuts can deeper into her backpack, but it was bulky, and she couldn't close the zipper. She realized now that she forgot her lunch. There was no going back, though. She couldn't take the risk.

Finally, Sam walked out. "You're early," Sam said just as Miles ran up.

"Come on, let's get out of here." Dottie darted away and Sam and Miles were forced to catch up.

"What's going on?" Miles asked.

"I'll tell you later," Dottie said.

"You have the can," Sam said.

"Not here," Dottie said. She didn't slow down until they were two blocks away.

Now that she was with Sam and Miles, she relaxed a little.

She had the can. If all went according to the mission, Dottie's life would now change.

"The can," Miles whispered like he was talking about gold. "Can I touch it?"

"Don't be gross," Dottie said.

"I didn't think you were going to bring it to school," Sam said, sounding worried.

"Me neither, but I'm making this up as I go along."

Dottie saw Miles's hand creeping closer. She slapped it away.

"You really won't let me touch it?"

Dottie ignored him.

"Do you think you'll get in trouble?" Sam asked. "If they find the can at school?"

Dottie hugged her backpack tighter. "They're not going to find it. We're the only ones who know I have it."

Miles said, "Your grandpa is going to be so sad when he realizes the can is missing."

"I can't believe you," Dottie said. "It was basically your idea."

"Um." Miles gulped. "I admit I had something to do with it, but I didn't think you would actually succeed."

Dottie scowled. "Well, what do I do now?"

"Hide it somewhere," Sam said.

"Where?" Dottie asked. "I mean, we're almost at school."

Miles nodded emphatically. "It also needs to be a really good hiding place since it will be there for a pretty long time."

"A pretty long time?" Dottie snapped. "You didn't say anything about a pretty long time."

"I didn't?" Miles asked.

"No," Dottie said. "You didn't."

"Oh, it took me three months to get over my PlayStation."

"Three months?!" Dottie was shocked. She couldn't wait three months to stop feeling sad.

"You never know," Miles said. "It might be faster. Whatever happens, you have to be strong. Not only for yourself but for Grandpa Walter."

"What do you mean for Grandpa Walter?"

"I know you're sad and he'll be really sad without the can, but you can't give in. You have to pretend you're a parent."

"A parent?" Sam asked.

Miles shrugged. "Parents never get sad about making us sad."

Sam nodded. "And, you've got to be sure no one finds the can."

Dottie gulped and tugged at the zipper, trying to close her

backpack. She had to close it. Right now, this was her only hiding place. She tugged and tugged and then tugged once more really hard and that's when the zipper broke.

"Oh no," Dottie said just as Ms. Agna smiled and waved them over.

44. What If?

Dottie lingered by the cubbies where the backpacks and coats dangled, hanging off their hooks. She grasped her backpack in one hand and the zipper in the other. What would she do now?

"Dottie?" Ms. Agna called from the rug. "Are you coming?"

"One second." Dottie waved from the cubbies. With the zipper broken, the Chock full o'Nuts can tumbled out of her backpack. Dottie fumbled with the can, looking for somewhere else to store it. Somewhere *not* in her backpack.

A knitted hat lay on the floor. Dottie grabbed the hat, stretching it over the Chock full o'Nuts can, and tucked the can on the floor where no one would see it.

Dottie gave the Chock full o'Nuts can one last look and then joined everyone else on the rug.

Because the Chock full o'Nuts can was hiding in the cubbies, Dottie struggled to concentrate. Somehow, she muscled through math, but then came reading responses, which took more focus. Ms. Agna asked them to write about something they wished for and then share with the class. Dottie had so many wishes (to banish her animals, to find a really good hiding spot, for Grandpa Walter to be happy, to finish the tree house) and some of them were top secret (the Chock full o'Nuts can), but most of all her biggest wish was to have Ima again. And that one hurt so much that she ended up doodling pictures of the animals storming inside her instead of writing words. Sometimes words were hard.

When they met back on the rug to share, Dottie hoped she wouldn't be called on. But it was fun to listen to the wishes of her schoolmates and she was impressed by them. Maggie wished to be a musician, Ivo wished to fight climate change, Steven wished to have a pet, Vita wished for equality, and Gerald wished to be a teacher, but when it was Miles's turn, he opened his journal and read, "Something I wish for is a home."

That got Dottie's attention. Miles had a home.

He read on. "Because my parents are getting a divorce, they have to sell our house. I don't know where I will live or if I will stay here."

What? Miles's family was moving? A million questions raced through her mind. Did Sam know? She looked at him, but he looked as shocked as she felt.

What if Miles moved away? What would life be like without him? Just imagining it made Dottie's stomach feel like a zoo. Miles could not move away. And not because a whole zoo was incredibly uncomfortable. No, it was because Dottie liked him. Dottie would miss him. Dottie's life would not be the same without him.

45. How Can That Be True?

"I don't want to talk about it," Miles said that afternoon while he, Sam, and Dottie were hunched over their bug posters, putting the final touches on the illustrations. The projects were taking longer than Ms. Agna planned because everyone loved them so much.

"What do you want to talk about, then?" Sam asked.

Miles smiled. "I want to talk about who would win in a battle between the strongest person in the world and the smartest person in the world." Before they could come to a final decision, though, Ivo leaped out of his seat and shouted, "Ms. Agna, it's recess!"

Ms. Agna looked up. "Oops! Late again! Everyone, it's recess and lunch!"

Suddenly, there was a mad scramble to the cubbies. And before Dottie could protect the can, Vita shouted, "Where's my hat?"

Dottie raced over, tunneling through the crowd. Was Vita's hat on the Chock full o'Nuts can?

"Never mind," Vita shouted again. "Found it." Dottie saw right away that it wasn't the same hat. Vita's was red. The can's hat was black. Dottie let out a deep sigh and then pushed her way closer to the can, guarding it until everyone was safely in line.

"Let's go!" Ms. Agna called as she led the class outside.

Strangely and without thinking, Dottie reached down and touched the can. Even though she knew it was silly, she couldn't help herself.

As they ran out for recess, Dottie's only thought was where to hide the can. Obviously, it couldn't stay at school under a hat for months and months. They raced over to the one tire swing on the playground, and settled down to brainstorm hiding places.

Backyard?

Basement?

Garage?

Sam's house?

Miles's house?

Under the bunk beds?

Nothing was right. As recess ended and lunch started, Miles said, "Could we take a break and play Truth or Fake instead?

"You want to play Truth or Fake?" Dottie asked, surprised.

Miles nodded. "My brain hurts from too much thinking. I need a distraction."

Dottie and Sam nodded. Their brains hurt too.

"Okay," Miles said. "Truth or fake? Our eyes see upside down."

"What?" Sam asked. "Upside down? That's got to be fake."

Miles looked at Dottie.

"I agree with Sam."

"You're both wrong. It's true." Miles nodded enthusiastically. "Our eyes see upside down and our brain turns it right way up."

"No," Dottie said. "How can that be true?"

"My dad showed it to me. In a book."

Sam frowned. "Why didn't anyone tell us about this sooner? I mean, if that's true, then what other stuff don't we know?"

Dottie said, "Ima used to say, there's more to life than meets the eye."

"My mom says that too," Miles said. "I never got it."

"Neither do I," Dottie said. "Until now." If nothing was the way Dottie saw it, did that mean she was wrong to take the can?

It was too late to wonder that. All Dottie could do was find a hiding spot and hope for the best.

46. Who Would Do Something Like That?

Dottie stood by the cubbies at the end of the day while Ms. Agna hustled the students to move along. She always said it was like herding cats (impossible)!

Sam and Miles stood on either side of Dottie. "What should I do?" she asked, pointing to the can, still hidden in the cubbies, under the hat.

Sam said, "You don't have any other place for it. It's safe here. At least for the weekend."

"I concur," Miles said. Dottie and Sam looked at him in total confusion. "*Concur* means to agree," Miles explained.

"I know what *concur* means," Sam said. "I'm just wondering why you said it."

Miles shrugged. "I'm trying to improve my vocabulary so it's as good as yours."

Dottie didn't like the idea of leaving the can, but she didn't have any other options. The can would have to stay at school for the weekend. Ms. Agna clapped her hands behind them. "Come on, time to go."

Dottie touched the can good-bye and trudged home with Sam. As soon as Dottie opened the front door, she wanted to turn and run away, but her dad rushed over, followed by her mom, and then Jazzy, blocking her escape.

"Oh Dottie," her dad said. "It's terrible."

The alligator's teeth scratched Dottie's insides.

Jazzy took over. "Ima is missing."

The kangaroo pounded on her heart.

"Ima's ashes," Dottie's dad corrected.

The octopus tightened around Dottie's throat.

"It's true," Dottie's mom said. "We can't find the can any-where."

"But-wha-wh-?" Dottie sputtered until she found some words. "Where would it go?"

"Exactly what I said." Dottie's mom nodded. "It couldn't just fly away."

The porcupine and bison rammed through Dottie's guts. She was lying to her family.

"Maybe someone stole it," Jazzy said.

"Who would do something like that?" Mom asked.

Dottie gulped.

"Who wouldn't?" Jazzy asked, looking shocked that her mom would ask that question. "The can is very important. And important things need to be protected or else they get stolen or lost like what happened to Purple Fish." (Purple Fish was

Jazzy's favorite stuffy that went missing a year ago. She was still very heartbroken.)

Dottie had never thought about it like that before. Jazzy was absolutely right. Important things did need to be protected. But what was more important, Dottie's heart or the Chock full o'Nuts can?

"Where's Grandpa Walter now?" Dottie asked.

"In bed," her mom said. "He won't get up."

Dottie's dad said, "I should have put the can on a shelf where it belonged."

"Frank, he needed it."

"He was protecting it," Jazzy said. "Because it is important."

Dottie's mom sighed. "I'm going to look in the basement."

"Why would it be there?" her dad asked.

"I don't know. But I've got to keep looking," she said, and ran down the stairs. Dottie's dad followed and Jazzy tagged along.

Dottie stayed behind wondering how long the search for the can would last and how long she could pretend she knew nothing about it.

47. Another Question?

Grandpa Walter spent the rest of Friday refusing to come out of his room.

Dottie paced the house. Jazzy hung upside down. Her mom corrected papers while her dad baked nonstop. This was what Dottie's dad did when he was upset. When Ima died, he baked so many cookies that they were eating them for weeks.

Dottie's mom turned to Dottie and said, "Dottie, you seem restless, how about bringing a cup of coffee to Grandpa Walter? I bet he'd like to see a fresh face and it'll give you something to do."

"I'll go!" Jazzy sat straight up with an arm raised high in the air like she was at school.

Dottie was fine with that. Every time she thought of seeing Grandpa Walter, the animals reminded her in their own unique ways that they were still there.

"I'd like Dottie to go." Her mom smiled.

Jazzy was about to argue but then their dad announced the cookies were done and Jazzy disappeared to gobble some up.

Dottie longed for a reason not to go but she didn't have one, so off she went with a cup of coffee and a cookie for Grandpa Walter.

Grandpa Walter was sitting up in bed, staring out the window when Dottie walked in. MacFurry, curled up in his lap, was purring. Dottie placed the coffee and cookie beside him, aware that it was only one cup and not two. The octopus clutched her heart and Dottie longed to get out of there as quickly as she could, but was stopped by Grandpa Walter, who turned to her. "What do you think happens when we die?" he asked.

The alligator crammed in her neck so she could only respond with a squeak. This was not the sort of question that grown-ups ever asked her and definitely not the sort of question she expected from Grandpa Walter (ever). Grandpa Walter didn't talk about this kind of thing. Of course, Dottie had thought about it before. Doesn't everyone? But no one ever talked about it, not even Ima.

"Really, Dottie," Grandpa Walter prodded. "I want to know what you think."

Death was scary and hard to put into words. But something about Grandpa Walter's question made the alligator in her belly wiggle away. Where did it go, Dottie wondered, and when would it come back? She shook her head and returned to Grandpa Walter's question. "I don't know, but it's certainly transformative."

"Transformative?" Grandpa Walter asked.

"It means we change from one form to another," Dottie said. Sam had taught her that years ago when they watched a caterpillar emerge from a chrysalis.

"Transformative," Grandpa Walter repeated. "Yes, it is." Grandpa Walter sighed. "What could have happened to her? Where did she go?" Dottie blinked. She sometimes wondered this about Ima too. Or was he talking about the can? Dottie wasn't sure.

Grandpa Walter sat up straighter and reached for the coffee. Then he stopped. "Oh, Dottie." Grandpa Walter sighed. "Who am I without Ima?"

"What do you mean?" Dottie asked.

Grandpa Walter looked down. "When you love someone so much, you become a part of them, and they become a part of you. And then"—Grandpa Walter's eyes met Dottie's—"they leave. And you have to keep doing everything you did except without them."

Dottie paused. Who would she be without her parents, or without Jazzy? Who would she be without Sam and now Miles? Who was she without Ima?

Who am I without Ima? Dottie repeated in her mind. The question felt too much, too big, and, without a doubt, too hard for her to answer.

48. Why Didn't We Think of That?

The next morning, Grandpa Walter's question stuck in her mind like the quills of the porcupine that was waddling around her insides.

Who was she without Ima?

Dottie hated this question. As far as she could see, there was no good answer. So she sprang out of bed, determined to get as far away from it as possible.

Luckily, Sam and Miles also wanted a distraction.

Sam didn't want to be at his house because there was a lot of baby stuff going on. Miles didn't want to be at his house because there was a lot of moving stuff going on. And clearly, Dottie didn't want to be home either. That's how they ended up at the school playground spending the entire day having staring contests, seeing who could hold their breath the longest, and playing hide-and-seek. And funnily enough, by the late afternoon, Dottie was feeling hopeful again. So hopeful, in fact, that she invited Sam and Miles back to the tree house.

Just to sit in it.

Dottie walked around the corner of her house, Sam and Miles followed, but a second later she came to a sudden and complete stop and then Sam crashed into her and Miles crashed into Sam. Dottie ignored them. She was rooted in place, gaping up at the tree house.

Dread. It was Sam's word, and she forgot what it meant exactly, but the sound of it perfectly described how she felt right now. Heavy, serious, and sad. Something had changed in the tree house but neither Dottie nor Sam nor Miles had changed it.

"You're home!" Grandpa Walter waved from above their heads. "At last!"

No. No. No. No. No. Grandpa Walter was supposed to be in his room—her room. Whatever. The point was: Grandpa Walter was not supposed to be in the tree house.

"What's he doing up there?" Miles asked.

"Does the tree house look different?" Sam asked.

"Did he do all this on his own?" Miles asked.

"Did he add walls?" Sam asked.

"And a roof?" Miles asked.

"And windows?" Sam asked.

"And a door?" Miles asked.

The questions were like zombies in a movie. They just kept

coming. And then Sam asked the question that tipped Dottie over the edge.

"Is that a bridge?" Sam asked. "From your window to the tree house?"

"Why didn't we think of that?" Miles asked.

I did, thought Dottie. *I just didn't have the chance to make it.*

49. How Many Questions?

Come on," Dottie ordered, scrambling up the rope ladder with Sam and Miles right behind.

Grandpa Walter waited at the top for them, beaming. It was the happiest Dottie had seen him in weeks, if not forever.

"Come inside." Grandpa Walter waved them into the room that Sam, Miles, and Dottie had left with two walls but now had four.

"What have you done?" Dottie asked, but no one heard her because they had all disappeared inside the room.

Dottie paused until she could see straight (she was pretty sure the octopus was swirling around in her head shooting out ink in every direction).

The first thing that caught her attention was MacFurry on a leash. Grandpa Walter pulled a face. "He wanted to follow me, so I had to do something."

Sam said, "So cute."

"Totally adorable," Miles added.

Dottie rolled her eyes.

Next, Dottie saw the painted walls. "The same green as my room," Grandpa Walter explained. "I had extra paint."

Sam said, "Nice."

Miles said, "I love green."

Dottie scowled.

Third, she saw curtains. "Ima always liked to have curtains on all the windows."

Sam said, "I hadn't thought about curtains."

Miles said, "Me neither."

Dottie clenched her fists.

Fourth, there was a table and two chairs. "I found them on the side of the road," Grandpa Walter explained.

"Those are from my house," Miles squeaked.

Sam comforted Miles with a gentle pat on the back.

And lastly, there was the bridge. "It just made sense." Grandpa Walter shrugged like constructing a bridge was nothing much.

Sam stared at the bridge longingly. "So cool."

Miles said, "Can I try it out?"

Dottie snarled. Luckily, she snarled quietly, so no one actually heard her. They also didn't hear (because she was too mad to speak) the burning question. HOW? HOW? HOW could Grandpa Walter have done all this in one day?

And as if Grandpa Walter heard her question, he said, "I don't know what got into me, but without Ima, I needed to do something. I couldn't sit around, pining for her. She would have hated that. Did you know, Dottie, that she always wanted a tree house?"

Dottie nodded in response to this question. Probably because the kangaroo had jammed itself down her throat, she was unable to make a sound.

50. Strawberry Shortcake?

Ⓗow did you do so much in a day?" Sam asked.

"You live as long as me and you pick up a few skills."

"I don't think I know anyone who could do this much," Sam added in awe.

Miles shrugged. "My dad could."

"Really?" Dottie heard the edge in Grandpa Walter's voice. Miles nodded.

"Well," Grandpa Walter said, rising to the challenge. "Can he do this?" And he reached into his mouth, gave a tug, and pulled out his set of false teeth.

Miles's eyes got big. "No," he said. "My dad definitely can't do that."

"Didn't think so," Grandpa Walter said, slipping his teeth back into place.

Grandpa Walter reached under the table and pulled out a cooler. "You want a snack?" he asked. Inside the cooler was a package of ice cream bars. "I've only got strawberry shortcake because they are the best."

Miles's face lit up. "My favorite!"

"Thanks," Sam said.

Dottie was not in the mood for a strawberry shortcake ice cream bar. This was her tree house. Not his! He had taken over her room and now the tree house. This was ridiculous. She would not allow it. She would stay here until he left.

Grandpa Walter pulled a deck of cards out of his pocket and shuffled. Who was he going to play cards with now? Ima was gone and so was the can. But he just laid the cards down in front of him. "Without Ima, I have to play solitaire. Some people call it *patience*. Did you know that?" he asked. "That's because it takes a lot of patience to play it and you usually lose."

Dottie watched him move the cards around until it was crystal clear that he was going nowhere. So Dottie left instead and dragged Sam and Miles along with her. (None of them used the bridge!)

51. A Cup of Coffee?

For the rest of the day, Dottie sat in her front yard, fiercely pulling at the grass. It infuriated her (Sam's word for super mad) that Grandpa Walter was so happy. But why? Wasn't that good? She had hoped when she took the can away that he would be happy too. But he was supposed to go away when he was happy, not stay and take over the tree house. She felt crummier than ever, which, considering how she had felt, was really saying something. But more than that, she just felt confused. So confused. Why was it so hard to be happy?

When it was close to dinner, Dottie's dad asked if she could find Grandpa Walter.

"Can't Jazzy do it?" Dottie asked. She had no interest in seeing Grandpa Walter or going anywhere near the tree house.

Dottie's dad shook his head. "She's having a bath."

"Before dinner?" Dottie said. Jazzy never took a bath before dinner.

"Let's say letting her play with the outside hose on her own was my big mistake."

By now Dottie's dad knew exactly where Grandpa Walter had spent the day and what he had done to her tree house. Still, he hadn't said anything to Dottie except "Don't worry. We will sort this out." To Dottie, it was clear that *this* was his big mistake. Instead of telling him that (what was the point?) she hauled herself out of the house and up the rope ladder. She was pulling herself onto the platform when she heard the sound.

A sound she had never heard come out of Grandpa Walter. Not even at Ima's funeral.

Creeping closer to the sound, Dottie found Grandpa Walter exactly where she had left him hours ago except back then he was playing cards and happy. Now MacFurry was curled up in his lap and he was sobbing big, drippy tears.

She wanted to sneak away—pretend she didn't see him crying—but her feet wouldn't move. There was only one reason he would be crying like this, and it was the same reason she would. Ima.

Dottie ached to hear Ima's laugh. To hear her shout "Surprise!" To be with her, sitting in the tree house, telling stories, and having fun. And without warning, Dottie couldn't hold it in anymore. First came the alligator, then the porcupine, then the octopus and then the kangaroo and last but not least, the bison. They all stampeded out and next came the tears.

Grandpa Walter looked up, startled by the noise. "Dottie," he said.

Dottie walked inside and crumpled into a chair beside Grandpa Walter. Tears spilled out of her.

When Dottie finally looked up, Grandpa Walter held out a handkerchief. She eyeballed it, not sure if she wanted it. "It's clean," he assured her.

Dottie blew her nose. Grandpa Walter sat very still.

"I miss Ima," Dottie said. "All the time."

"I know you do," Grandpa Walter said.

"I don't like being sad," she said. "It hurts."

"It does," Grandpa Walter said. "It feels like wild animals have moved in."

Dottie laughed. He felt that way too?

"Luckily, emotions are like a cup of coffee."

"A cup of coffee?" Dottie asked. "What's that mean?"

Grandpa Walter explained. "I'm the cup. The coffee is the emotion. I'm full of sadness until I start drinking it. Then it goes away."

Dottie thought about this. "You're the cup and the person drinking out of the cup at the same time?"

"Yup."

"And the coffee is the sadness?"

"Not the best metaphor, I admit."

"And sadness fills you up and then goes away?"

"That's it. Mind you, the coffee can be any emotion. It could be happiness too. It all goes up and down."

"Why?" asked Dottie. "Why can't it just be happy?"

Grandpa Walter thought. "We can't feel happiness without

also feeling sadness. I wouldn't feel sad if I didn't have so much happiness with Ima and I wouldn't give up my time with Ima just because I feel sad now. I will never stop loving her. I will never stop missing her. And still, I will be happy again. Like today. Like right now."

Dottie thought about this. "What do you think of out of sight, out of mind?"

"A load of hooey."

"Why is it a load of hooey?"

Grandpa Walter shrugged. "People are in such a rush. They want us to ignore our feelings and move on as fast as we can—especially when we're sad. Why?"

"Because they want you to be happy."

"It doesn't work that way. It's not like turning off a light switch and you stop feeling something. We all need time."

Dottie thought about this. If Grandpa Walter was right, then Dottie was wrong. What she needed had nothing to do with a tree house or the can. She needed time. Like Grandpa Walter.

Dottie paused and did the thing that she hadn't done when he first came. She did the thing she had never done and the thing he never asked for. She held his hand.

And he held her hand back.

"I love you, Grandpa Walter," Dottie said.

"You do?" Grandpa Walter asked. Dottie squeezed his hand tight to prove that she did, and he squeezed back to prove that he loved her.

52. What's Ima-ing?

Dottie spent her Sunday hiding in the top bunk. Alone. Thinking through everything that Grandpa Walter had talked about last night.

She was in the middle of a dilemma (Sam's word). Usually the word made her giggle, but this problem was too serious to giggle about.

All this time, she had been trying to get rid of her sadness and it didn't seem to be working. She still felt miserable, but now she also felt miserable about taking the can. She knew Miles would tell her it would take time and, funny enough, Grandpa Walter said the same thing. Time. Everything took time.

But there was something else. Something missing. Something Dottie was missing.

Inside her the animals crashed around—scratching, clawing, prodding. She wanted them gone, but she was too worn out to fight them. Normally when she felt this exhausted—after a long day at school or a fight with Jazzy—she might scream or cry or even kick. Unlike most grown-ups, Ima never got mad. Instead, she'd scooped Dottie up and held her. Tight and safe and secure.

Dottie sat up; maybe she did know what was missing.

If someone had asked Dottie what she was doing, she might have said that she was Ima-ing. And when that someone asked what's Ima-ing, Dottie wouldn't have the words to explain it.

But Dottie started with the alligator, moved on to the porcupine, then the octopus and kangaroo and ended with the bison. Holding each one tightly, safely, and securely. And, as she did, she discovered that, like Miles and Grandpa Walter, the animals were not as bad as she thought.

Suddenly, like the sun poking out behind a cloud, Dottie knew what to do about the can. Now she just had to wait until the next day—Monday—to do it.

53. How Could I Remember That?

Dottie woke up feeling exuberant. *Exuberant* was the word Sam used to describe feeling really, really happy. It was funny to think that she felt happy doing something that would make her sad. But, then again, life was weird.

Sam and Miles were already waiting outside when she ran out the door to meet them.

She took a deep breath and told them her decision. "I'm returning the can to Grandpa Walter."

Both Sam and Miles got really quiet.

Dottie continued. "He needs the can more than I don't." And even though that made no sense at all, it was true.

She waited for one of them to speak. At last, Sam said, "Wow. That's majestic."

"Majestic," Miles repeated. "Truly majestic."

Dottie was positive that, at last, they were using the word correctly.

Now that Dottie had a plan about the Chock full o'Nuts can, she was impatient for school to start and end. "How the heck am I going to get through a whole entire day?"

Right away Sam said, "The good news is you'll get it back sooner than on a normal day."

"Why?" Dottie asked.

"It's a half day. Remember? They sent a note home on Friday."

"How could I remember that with everything else going on?" Dottie asked.

"I forgot too," Miles admitted. "I've got a lot on my mind." He sounded really sad.

"Miles," Sam said. "No matter where you live, we will always be friends."

"It's true," Dottie agreed. She couldn't imagine life without Miles.

Dottie was over the moon when she found the Chock full o'Nuts can right where she left it on Friday. Hidden under the hat. Being over the moon meant that she was happy. She liked that expression and was glad that Sam had taught it to her.

As Dottie suspected, the day wore on in a slow and distracted way. Dottie was also over the moon that it was only a half day because if it had been a whole one, she would certainly have been under the moon.

Finally, it was time for recess and lunch and after lunch they went home. Dottie had made it.

"Don't forget to bring your backpacks with you," Ms. Agna reminded them.

Dottie waited until everyone had collected their bags and then scooped up the Chock full o'Nuts can, pulled the hat off, and stuffed the can into her backpack. The zipper was still broken, but she didn't worry about it. She was bringing the can home, where it belonged.

Recess flew by with a game of Truth or Fake, the speed round. This version consisted of Sam, Miles, and Dottie shouting out truths or fakes as fast as they could.

"Truth or fake? A chicken is a dinosaur." (Truth.)

"Truth or fake? Baby camels are called camelettes." (Fake.)

"Truth or fake? If you get chased by an alligator, don't run in a straight line." (Truth.)

"Truth or fake? Seaweed is actually a weed." (Fake.)

"Truth or fake? When you get sucked into a black hole you pop out in a different universe." (No one knows.)

When the recess bell rang, they all ran in for lunch.

Mr. Shark looked as shark-like as ever, but Dottie ignored him. There was more to life than Mr. Shark, and she wasn't going to let him ruin her day.

54. You Want Help With That?

Miles pulled out a thermos from his lunch. He grunted and groaned as he struggled with the lid.

"You want help with that?" Dottie asked.

"No, I got it." He paused, took a deep breath, and then twisted hard. The thermos flew out of his hands; the lid shot one way and the soup another. Dottie leaped up with a napkin for Miles just as Mr. Shark circled around.

"Dottie Bing!" Mr. Shark called out. "What are you doing out of your seat?"

"Miles spilled his soup. I was giving him a napkin."

"That's not your job," Mr. Shark said.

"I know," Dottie said, exasperated. "But Mr. Shark, it's just nice to help."

Mr. Shark strode to the side of the room and grabbed a bucket of soapy water used for accidents like this. He reached in and pulled out a washcloth. "Miles spilled it. Miles cleans it."

Mr. Shark watched him. "You missed some." Mr. Shark pointed under the table, right next to Dottie's backpack. Miles reached farther to clean up all the soup.

Mr. Shark squinted. "What's that?" He pointed to the Chock full o'Nuts can that poked out of her backpack.

"It's mine," Dottie said, trying to grab it quickly.

"Why are you bringing coffee to school, Miss Bing?"

"It's not coffee."

Sam frantically shook his head back and forth. "Don't—"

"If it's not coffee, what is it?" Mr. Shark frowned.

"Uh," Dottie said. "It belongs to my grandfather."

"Why are you bringing something that belongs to your grandfather that isn't coffee to school?"

"It's a long story."

"I've got time."

"It's complicated."

"Dottie Bing," Mr. Shark said. "Open that can at once."

Sam's eyes opened wide. Miles's opened even wider.

Dottie froze.

"Open the can. If it's not coffee inside, I want to see what it is."

Dottie shook her head.

"Open it."

"I can't open it."

Mr. Shark crossed his arms. "I've had quite enough of this. Open the can this instant."

Dottie didn't know what she was more afraid of, Mr. Shark or opening the can.

"Fine," Mr. Shark said. Dottie breathed a sigh of relief. Mr. Shark was coming to his senses. "I'll open it."

Dottie looked on in horror as Mr. Shark started to pull off the plastic lid. How could there be such a flimsy lid on such an important can? She had never thought about this before. It should be much harder to get into a can of someone's ashes. There should be a lock on it, or it should be sealed shut. But a plain old plastic lid? Whose idea was that?

"Stop!" Dottie shouted. "STOP!"

Dottie reached up and grabbed the can as Mr. Shark jerked the can back and pulled off the lid.

For one second, he looked triumphant, but then he stepped

in a small puddle of Miles's spilled soup, and that's when he lost all control, his foot slipped out from under him, and he crashed to the ground as the Chock full o'Nuts can tumbled out of his hands and flipped over in the air twice. The entire contents rained down all over him.

55. What Do You Mean, "Ima's Ashes"?

Mr. Shark lay on the ground, his face covered in Ima.

The room became very still.

And then Miles shouted, "Ima! You've got Ima's ashes all over your face!" Miles's hands popped straight over his mouth. He looked at Dottie.

Mr. Shark's eyes got very big. "What do you mean 'Ima's ashes'?"

Dottie's eyes got big too. "It's my fault," she said, her voice shaking. "It's all my fault."

"Dottie Bing." Mr. Shark slowly got up. "What is this about ashes?"

"The Chock full o'Nuts can," Dottie said. "It holds my grandma's—" Sam interrupted her. "Coffee. You spilled her grandma's favorite coffee all over you."

Dottie looked at Sam Batty. She was totally confused.

"Miles said it was ashes," Mr. Shark hissed. "Dottie Bing, did you bring the ashes of your grandmother to school?"

Sam carried on as if everything was normal. "Dottie would never do that. Look at it. Even you can tell the difference between coffee grounds and ashes."

Now everyone, including Dottie, looked. And without a doubt, it was definitely coffee.

56. How Could Dottie Explain It?

All the students had gone home except Dottie, who was still in the principal's office. Although it was only coffee, Mr. Shark insisted that she stay and clear this up.

Sam and Miles had already been interviewed and were home now.

Dottie sat with Ms. Agna waiting for Grandpa Walter, who had been called since both Dottie's parents were working.

Ms. Agna was saying, "I don't understand why you brought the Chock full o'Nuts can to school." How could Dottie explain? She didn't even know where to start, and when she tried to it all got blocked by the bison's bottom. At least that was how it felt to Dottie.

And right then Grandpa Walter rushed in. He saw the can and stopped.

"I'm sorry," Dottie said, blinking back tears. She hated crying. "It was a mistake, a big mistake. I'd even call it a blunder."

Dottie used Sam's word so Grandpa Walter would know she was serious.

Grandpa Walter sat down.

"Dottie," Ms. Agna said. "Maybe you could start at the beginning for your grandfather and me."

Dottie took a deep breath and the whole story tumbled out. How sad she was and all the questions she asked to make the sadness go away and how she was sure building a tree house would help because it's what Ima wanted. And then she explained about taking the can. "I thought out of sight, out of mind would make me feel better. But I was wrong. Maybe some problems can be fixed by that, but not mine. And not Grandpa Walter's."

Grandpa Walter still hadn't said a word. Dottie wondered if he would ever speak to her again. She was so scared about this that she didn't ask how coffee ended up in the Chock full o'Nuts can instead of Ima's ashes. She didn't even ask the really big question: If Ima's ashes weren't in the Chock full o'Nuts can, then where were they?

There was a knock on the door and Principal Knight walked in. She sat at her desk. "First, I want to thank you for coming in, Mr. Bing. And for explaining about the Chock full o'Nuts can to us over the phone. I can honestly say we were happy to hear that it was coffee . . . especially Mr. Park."

Grandpa Walter stood up. "I'm afraid this is my blunder."

Dottie looked at Grandpa Walter.

"Excuse me?" Principal Knight said.

"Dottie wanted to help me. It's entirely my fault. Would you tell Mr. Park how sorry I am?"

Principal Knight sighed. "I think Mr. Park was a bit over-zealous in his duty."

Dottie liked that word: *overzealous*. She'd have to tell Sam about it when she saw him again. If she ever saw him again.

Ms. Agna turned to Principal Knight. "After Dottie's explanation, I suggest that perhaps it's time to let her go home."

"Really?" Dottie asked.

Principal Knight nodded. "You two seem to have figured it out, yes?"

As Grandpa Walter and Dottie walked out, Principal Knight stopped them. "Don't forget this." She handed Grandpa Walter the empty Chock full o'Nuts can.

As they left the building, Mr. Park was leaving too. Grandpa Walter pulled Dottie off to the side. "I think we're the last people he wants to see."

Mr. Park's clothes were covered in a thin cloud of coffee grains. He did not look happy, but then again, he never looked happy. It reminded Dottie of MacFurry. Maybe someday he could change. But, like with MacFurry, Dottie was not the one who was going to change him.

57. Where's Ima?

Dottie and Grandpa Walter were walking to Grandpa Walter's car when he stopped and pointed to a bench beside them. "Can we sit a minute?" he asked, settling down on it before Dottie answered. Grandpa Walter paused. "I should have told everyone what was in the can, but I felt so bad."

Dottie didn't know what to say, so she didn't say anything.

"You know, Ima never liked a fuss. She did ask to go into a Chock full o'Nuts can. But she also asked that I scatter a small amount of her ashes in Piney Pond. It was only going to be a small amount. A handful. I opened the can and then—well, you know what I'm like—I tripped."

"You tripped?"

"The can went flying and so did Ima's ashes. All of them. Scattered. Everywhere."

"Does Daddy know?"

Grandpa Walter shook his head. "I felt terrible. I mean,

Ima wouldn't care. You know she would think it was funny."

Dottie nodded. Ima would have *definitely* thought that was funny.

"But your dad—" He broke off and slumped his head.

"So, you filled the can with coffee so he wouldn't know?"

Grandpa Walter nodded. "At first I was pretending and then soon it didn't matter that it wasn't her. To me, it felt like Ima was there." Grandpa Walter tapped on the can.

Dottie understood lots about pretending. She pretended too. Pretended she was fine with Grandpa Walter sleeping in her room, painting her room, taking over the tree house. Pretended that her emotions were animals. Pretended that it was the can, not Ima, that made her sad. Pretending wasn't always a bad thing. "And so even though it isn't her," Dottie said, wrapping her brain around this, "you feel like she's there. And that's why you talk to her and carry her around and play cards with her and give her a cup of coffee?"

Grandpa Walter nodded. "I know it doesn't make sense, but I do. I feel like she's there." Grandpa Walter let out a deep sigh that lasted longer than Dottie imagined any sigh could, then he said, "Dottie, there's something I have to confess. Ima never suggested I should paint your room. It was me. All me."

"Why did you say it was her?"

"Because she and I always had green in our house. I wanted to feel close."

Dottie shook her head. "No, I mean why didn't you explain that *you* wanted it green?"

"I thought you would say no."

Dottie frowned. In a way, Grandpa Walter was right, but in a way he was wrong. "I said yes because it's what Ima would have done." Also, Dottie didn't really mind the color.

Grandpa Walter smiled. "Ima always loved the blue color of your room. She said it made her happy."

She was glad that Ima liked her blue room. For a little while more they sat on the bench in silence. Dottie kicked around in her brain everything that had been said. Then she asked, "Does she talk to you at all?"

Grandpa Walter nodded. "She does. She tells me she loves me. She tells me I'll get through this." He paused. "She told me to come live with you."

Dottie nodded. "Ima always had good ideas."

"Ima had all the ideas," Grandpa Walter said. "Without her, I don't know what to do."

"But without Ima, you built the tree house," Dottie reminded him.

Grandpa Walter laughed. "Without you, the tree house wouldn't have been built."

Dottie smiled. "Without Ima, I never would have built the tree house."

"Without Ima, none of us would be here."

"Wow." Dottie blinked. She hadn't thought about that before, but it was so true. "Life is majestic," she said.

"Majestic?" Grandpa Walter asked. He didn't know what she was talking about.

"It's something Sam and Miles and I say."

Grandpa Walter looked confused. Dottie felt the same way. It was like she was trying to untie a knot with her words. "If it wasn't for life, then you and Ima never would have met, and if you and Ima never met, then Dad would never have been born, and if Dad had never been born, then he and Mom wouldn't have met, and if he and Mom had never met, then I would never have been born and I would never have known you." Her brain hurt after thinking about all that.

Grandpa Walter stood up. "Dottie, you are right. Life *is* majestic. That's exactly what Ima would say." He took Dottie's hand and pulled her up. He was stronger than he looked.

And in that moment, Dottie's heart grew a million times bigger. Sort of like five animals had squeezed into it and instead of clogging, poking, prodding, squeezing, or jumping, they simply wanted to cuddle.

58. You Know What This Means?

Two days ago, when Dottie and Grandpa Walter arrived home with the empty can, the whole story was told again. Dad didn't take it well, but Dottie made Grandpa Walter hug him and he seemed better. Grandpa Walter and Dottie's dad and mom went out into the tree house for a private talk. When they got back, the whole family sat down.

Dad explained to Dottie and Jazzy that Grandpa Walter was staying.

Jazzy exploded out of her seat. "YES!" she hollered. "Grandpa Walter is staying! This is just what I wanted!"

Dottie was glad too, even if it meant sharing a room with Jazzy for the rest of her life.

Her parents went on to say that they had decided Dottie needed her room back and so Grandpa Walter and Jazzy would share.

"Yes!" Jazzy shouted, and leaped into Grandpa Walter's

arms. "Do you want the top bunk or the bottom? You can choose."

Grandpa Walter, though, had a different idea. He was going to build a wall down the middle of Jazzy's room, so the one room became two.

Jazzy was excited about this too. "We can bang to each other. It'll be like tap-dancing with our hands."

Grandpa Walter looked a little worried about this. "Just remember, Jazzy, Grandpa Walter likes his quiet."

A few minutes later, the phone rang. When her mom hung up, she said. "Dottie, would you go outside? Sam's waiting for you."

Dottie shrugged, confused by what her mom was talking about. She didn't have a plan to meet Sam.

Outside, Sam stood with his mom. Sam was smiling and his hand pressed against his mom's belly, which looked like she had swallowed a kangaroo.

"What's going on?" Dottie asked Sam when he ran over to her.

"I don't know," Sam said. "But I just felt the baby move. And I've decided to follow your lead."

"What lead is that?" Dottie asked.

"To choose to be majestic instead of sad."

Dottie smiled. "We'll be able to teach the baby all about zombies."

"And Truth and Fake," Sam said.

"And tree houses."

A car drove up right then, followed by a large van with the words *Moving Buddies* written across it.

The car doors opened, and Miles Huckatony stepped out. Dottie was confused. Was Miles moving away? Had he come to say goodbye?

"Truth or fake?" Miles asked Dottie and Sam. "Zombie House has zombies."

"Don't you dare say fake," Dottie said. "I saw a zombie in there. I know I did."

"Fake!" Miles shouted. "Fake! Fake! Fake! You saw my mom!"

"What?" Dottie said. "Your mom is a zombie?"

"No! My mom bought it."

"Bought it?" Sam said. "Bought Zombie House?"

"It was my mom that Dottie saw. She didn't tell me because she wasn't sure it would work out."

"You're moving into Zombie House?" Dottie asked.

"Yeah," Miles said. "Except it's not Zombie House anymore. It's Huckatony House."

"You're going to be our neighbor?" Sam said.

"Yes!" Miles said, and he started to dance.

"You're going to live right across the street?" A huge smile filled Dottie's face.

"How many times do I need to say it?" Miles asked.

"You know what this means?" Dottie closed her hands into excited fists.

"What?" Miles asked.

"I know what it means," Sam said, nodding his head.

"Will someone please tell me what it means?" Miles said.

"Should we tell him?" asked Dottie.

"I don't know, do you think he can handle it?" Sam asked.

"I can handle it," Miles said. "I can handle anything."

"I don't know," Dottie said. "Maybe we should wait."

"We could wait," Sam said.

"JUST TELL ME!" Miles hollered.

Sam and Dottie looked at each other.

"Would you like to tell him?" Dottie asked Sam.

"Oh no, you tell him, I insist," Sam said.

"TELL ME WHAT?!" Miles hollered again.

Dottie took a deep breath and said, "Now we can build a tree house in your tree!"

Miles's face lit up. "That's a good tree for a tree house."

"It's perfect," Sam said. "In fact, it's been waiting for us all its life. Hasn't it, Dottie?"

"Yes, Sam, yes it has. And now—" Dottie sighed deeply. "There's only one question left."

"What's that?" Miles asked.

"Where did the zombies go after they left your house?"

Miles shook his head. "They didn't go anywhere because there never were zombies in the house."

"Are you sure?" Sam asked. "Have you looked in the basement?"

"No," Miles said, and frowned. "Do you think we should?"

Dottie shrugged. "You know what Ima always said: Every solution starts with a question."

Miles said, "Nothing personal Dottie, but sometimes I don't understand you."

"Welcome to the club." Sam laughed.

As Dottie, Sam, and Miles walked up to the house, Dottie realized that there was no end to questions. There were millions and millions of them just waiting to be asked. Sometimes she'd ask the hard ones and sometimes she'd ask easy ones. Sometimes she'd answer them correctly and sometimes she'd answer them wrong. The point was to keep asking because asking questions was always more interesting than not.

Luckily, right now, the question was obvious: What was in the basement?

There might be zombies. There might not. But there was only one way to answer that question.

Miles opened the front door and they all walked in.

Acknowledgments

QUESTION: Truth or fake? Writing a book is like building a tree house. ANSWER: Truth.

And like a tree house, you need a tree. These people are the tree for my tree house. They are the roots, the trunk, and the limbs. They are the leaves, the bark, the seeds, and the sap. I give thanks every day for their unwavering support and belief.

Thank you, Molly O'Neill, my tremendous agent, whose faith, wisdom, and love of story kept me writing during the tough times. Thank you to the team at Root Literary agency who care for their artists with passion and smarts. Thank you, Ellen Cormier, my visionary, brilliant, and patient editor. This book would not be here without you. (Not joking!) Thank you to the entire extraordinary and caring team at Dial Books for Young Readers: Jen Klonsky, publisher; Nancy Mercado, editorial director; Regina Castillo, copy editor; Tabitha Dulla, managing editor; Sylvia Bi, interior designer; Jess Jenkins, cover designer; and Squish Pruitt, editorial assistant. Dottie and I are truly lucky to have found our home with you.

Thank you to Fanny Liem, the incredible illustrator, for her creativity and art. Thank you to my outstanding family: my mom (Sophy), pop (David), stepmom (Joanne), hubby (Sean), two kids (Adelaide and Georgia), sister (Sarah), niece and nephew (Bea and Soap), Pepito (dog), and Gesar (cat), who kept me company, inspired me, and cheered me on through every draft and every revision. Thank you to the marvelous Mojos (Jackie Davies, Leslie Connor, Lita Judge, Ali Benjamin, and Grace Lin), and my phenomenal friends Eliza Factor, Kate Samworth, Diane Thomas, Charlie Bell, and Ivo and Vita, Yolanda Hare, Libby Nehill, Lucinda Oakes, and Mike Curato. Thank you to teachers and librarians. Thank you to the LGBTQIA community. Thank you to the communities that question and push me to be a better human being. And lastly, I'd like to thank trees. Without them, there would be no tree houses, and more importantly, there would be no air. Trees are awesome.